BUSHWHACKED

IN THE

OUTBACK

A LAND SHARKS COZY MYSTERY ADVENTURE

BUSHWHACKED
IN THE
OUTBACK

A LAND SHARKS COZY MYSTERY ADVENTURE
(Book 2)

by

NANCY RAVEN SMITH

Whimsey Wylde
Santa Monica, California

DEDICATION

To Brad Smith

My Hero

CONTENTS

Title Page iii
Copyright iv
Dedication v
Contents vi
Map of Australia viii

Chapter One 1
Chapter Two 7
Chapter Three 13
Chapter Four 21
Chapter Five 31
Chapter Six 37
Chapter Seven 41
Chapter Eight 49
Chapter Nine 55
Chapter Ten 63
Chapter Eleven 77
Chapter Twelve 87
Chapter Thirteen 93
Chapter Fourteen 101
Chapter Fifteen 107
Chapter Sixteen 109
Chapter Seventeen 111
Chapter Eighteen 117
Chapter Nineteen 123

CONTENTS

Chapter Twenty 137
Chapter Twenty-One 141
Chapter Twenty-Two 147
Chapter Twenty-Three 155
Chapter Twenty-Four........................ 165
Chapter Twenty-Five 171
Chapter Twenty-Six 181
Chapter Twenty-Seven 189
Chapter Twenty-Eight 195
Chapter Twenty-Nine 199
Chapter Thirty 203
Chapter Thirty-One 209
Chapter Thirty-Two 213
Chapter Thirty-Three 223
Chapter Thirty-Four 227
Chapter Thirty-Five 237
Chapter Thirty-Six 239
Chapter Thirty-Seven....................... 243

Acknowledgements 247
Books By Nancy Raven Smith 248
Interesting Facts About Coober Pedy, AU .. 250
About The Author........................... 252

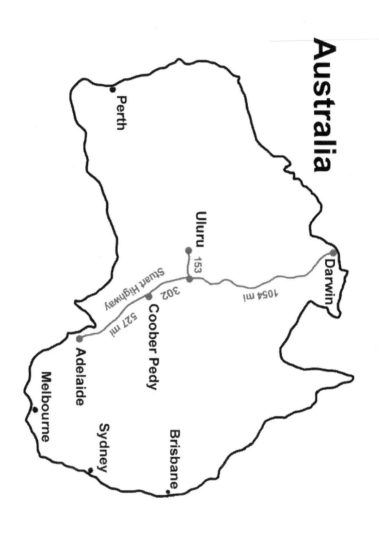

Australia

Perth

Uluru

153

Stuart Highway

302

1054 mi

Darwin

527 mi

Coober Pedy

Adelaide

Melbourne

Sydney

Brisbane

CHAPTER ONE

"I've been robbed!" A woman shrieks at the top of her lungs.

Her words echo around my office located on the mezzanine above the Bank of Beverly Hills' lobby.

I press the police alarm button under my desk and reach in the bottom drawer for my Glock. Racing into the hall in an adrenaline rush, I look over the railing to the lower floor.

Below, customers are fleeing out the entrance. Unfortunately, I can't see what's going on from here. I dash to the stairs and hurry down.

At the bottom, I take a deep breath, then slowly open the lobby door, hoping to size up the robbers before confronting them.

Nearby tellers are peering over their counters in the direction of the open cubicles where the managers and loan officers work. I turn in that direction.

The source of the shrieking? A stout, grey-haired woman in her sixties yelling, "I've been robbed," at the top of her lungs.

Tina, the young, assistant loan manager looks like a deer caught in the headlights and Bud Rodgers, the senior security officer, tries to calm the screaming woman.

Slipping my gun in my pocket, I emerge from the stairwell, and approach them.

"Can I be of any assistance?" I ask.

The grey-haired woman pauses mid-screech and turns in my direction. Tina makes use of the lull to say, "This is Lexi Winslow. She's in our fraud department and I'm sure she can help you." She adds, "Lexi, this is Bibi Adams, one of our customers."

Mrs. Adams looks me up and down.

I let her look. I'm thirty-four, five foot eight with an athletic build and sandy blonde hair. I consider myself average looking. Although I've been called fashion challenged by friends, today the conservative navy suit and print top I'm wearing are totally appropriate for my job.

I do cringe a little when Mrs. Adams pauses at my feet. Opps. I ran out in such a hurry I'm still wearing the fluffy, lime green crocodile slippers from my office.

Mrs. Adams gives me a contemptuous look.

Okay, so the slippers aren't appropriate. But since I rarely deal directly with the bank's customers, I keep them under my desk to wear when I'm alone, working on my computer.

Having dismissed me, Mrs. Adams starts to bluster again.

A fleeting image of a circus steam calliope pops into my head.

"Please, Mrs. Adams. That's not helping," Bud says. "Let's see what Lexi can do."

"I want the person in charge. I want my money."

Real sirens blare as the Beverly Hills Police arrive. The noise is deafening.

Guns drawn, the police swarm the bank. The sight of the weapons pointed in her direction chokes Mrs. Adams to silence.

I wave my friend, Detective Jeff Corbin, over to apologize and explain the misunderstanding. There are no robbers, just one very upset woman. Luckily Jeff and I have a long history, plus he's the world's nicest guy. We graduated from the L.A. Police Academy together, before I changed my career to bank fraud and forensic accounting.

After I finish explaining the situation, Jeff gives Mrs. Adams a hard stare, reads her the riot act by comparing her actions to yelling "fire" in a crowded theater. Then he and Tina head off to deal with the paperwork involved. As he passes me he whispers, "Love the slippers."

I ignore him. He doesn't know that I had to buy these slippers when I saw them because they reminded me of an incident I was involved in last year with a crocodile.

I turn to Mrs. Adams. "Please come with me and let's see what we can do about your problem."

Walking her to the elevator, I feel pretty silly in my slippers now. Behind my back, one of the employees snickers. It's followed by a second snicker from a policeman. Lifting my chin, I keep walking.

On the second floor, I lead Mrs. Adams toward my office. But I change my mind. My office is not a good place for a customer of the bank. I pass it and continue on to the conference room.

Once seated, Mrs. Adams immediately complains, "This bank has stolen all my money. I want it back now."

A quick look at her account on the conference room computer tells me her problem. Unfortunately, it's a common one.

"Did you write a check for four hundred dollars to Roman's Groceries last month?" I read from her bank statement.

"Definitely not," she blusters. "I shop at Better Foods."

"Or one for three hundred and sixty to Witman's Department Store?"

"No."

"Here's what's happened to your money. A thief got hold of your checking account number, printed duplicate checks using your number, and has cashed them at different stores. Quite a few of them. Once they emptied your checking account, the overdraft protection you signed up for kicked in and took money out of your savings account to pay for the overdrafts. Once your savings account was drained, the fake checks kept coming. That made your own checks bounce and the bank started charging overdraft fees."

"That can't be right. No, this is all the bank's fault. There's no way I'm overdrawn. I'm very careful about my records. It's time to pay my bills. I want my money."

"Don't worry. Here's what we'll do. First, we'll close this account. We'll recall copies of all your checks from our records for last month. You can come in and identify all the ones you didn't write. Once we verify that, we'll refund those amounts to you in a new account. And we'll remove all the overdraft fees and put out fraud alerts. But it may take a week or two."

Mrs. Adams thinks about it.

"What I am going to suggest so this doesn't happen again," I say, "is that I'll open a new checking account and savings account for you, but I won't connect them. No overdraft protection. Then if anyone breaks into your checking account again, they'll have no access to your savings. Do you have trouble with overdrawing your account?"

"Never."

"Then paying an occasional overdraft fee will be better than losing all your savings."

We arrange a time for her to come back, and I escort

her out. Mini crisis over.

I don't mention that I wish banks would warn people about this possibility if they choose overdraft protection.

Still, this is the part of my job as a bank fraud investigator I love best - helping people who've been victims of white collar crime. The police have their days filled with crimes against persons, and not enough manpower to deal with crimes against property. Identity theft and scam artists are at the bottom of their to-do list.

I get the frustration people have. I've seen first-hand how devastating white collar crimes can be to a family.

My friend, the detective, waits next to the lobby elevator. I'd forgotten how physically handsome Jeff is. In his mid-thirties, he still maintains the muscular body from his days as an amateur boxer in the Navy.

"Haven't heard from you in a bit," Jeff says.

"I've been traveling a lot on bank business."

"How about dinner tonight and catching up?"

CHAPTER TWO

Jeff wants to try the trendy, upscale Lombardi Restaurant in Beverly Hills for dinner. Since my alternative was a frozen dinner in front of the television, I'm happy with his choice.

Jeff and I place our orders of lasagne and gnocchi. I'm surprised when Jeff requests a bottle of my favorite Chianti for us to split. He's normally a craft beer guy.

After the waiter leaves, Jeff leans closer, takes my hand in his, and says, "I've been thinking about us a lot lately and about the future --"

That's when I realize that there's something different going on with him tonight. And it's the last thing I ever expected.

Is he proposing to me?

By the time I fully realize his intentions, he's already reached the "Lexi, I have an important question to ask you" point.

Before he can finish, I interrupt him by accidentally bumping my purse off the table as a distraction. The contents, including my Glock, scatter across the floor.

He spots the gun. Alarmed, Jeff drops his napkin over it and bends down quickly to retrieve it before anyone notices. While he's occupied under the table, my hand hastily slides to the phone in my pocket and hits the ring button. My phone rings immediately. The 1812 Overture, loudly echoes throughout the restaurant.

Chatter dies. Annoyed diners turn to stare. On the far side of the room, the head of the stuffy maitre d' swivels in our direction with a scowl on his face.

I pretend to answer the phone. "Lexi here...Yes?...Can't it wait?...Okay, I'll be right there."

I hang up as the angry maitre d' arrives at my side. "No phone, Madam," he hisses in my ear with a phony French accent and turns away.

Actually, it's mademoiselle, and why he's adopting a fake French accent in an Italian restaurant is beyond me. But I'm too occupied trying to divert Jeff to correct him.

Conversations slowly resume around the room.

Jeff sits back in his chair and slides my purse to me. He's tucked my Glock inside. "You brought a gun to dinner?" he asks, unable to hide the annoyance in his voice.

"Do I detect a bulge under your arm?"

"That's different."

"Okay for you, but not me? That's a bit of a double standard."

"Let's not do this. There's no reason a forensic accountant needs a gun. And your bank has it's own security team."

"Jeff, I'm really sorry, but I have to go. A problem at work."

I'm already jumping out of my chair as I speak. I snatch up my purse and shove my phone into it.

"I'll drive you," he says.

"No, you stay. Enjoy your dinner. By the time you get your car out of the garage, it'll be quicker if I walk. It's only two blocks."

With that, I beat the hastiest retreat ever committed by a woman in the history of the universe.

Halfway to the door, I pause. Remorse hits me. I glance back at Jeff. He's frozen, standing next to the table, with a stunned expression.

Is this the worst thing I've ever done? Probably not, but it sure feels like it. Jeff deserves better. I do love him, but not romantically. Somewhere the perfect woman is waiting for him. It's just not me.

I manage a tepid wave before I gallop past the aggravated maitre d' to escape through the front door onto busy Rodeo Drive.

"Cab, miss?" The curbside valet asks.

I nod. I'll need one since I'm really headed home to

Santa Monica and not to the bank nearby.

That was a close call with Jeff. I missed all the clues. The expensive restaurant, his serious demeanor, even the fact he wore a suit and tie which he hates.

If I refuse his proposal, will it end our friendship? I'd hate that.

At the moment, I'm not open to a romance. There is a man that I have feelings for. A man I learned too late not to put my trust in. He used me and left me in a mess. With any luck, I'll never see him again. Unfortunately I do still think about him. His touch is burned in my memory. That's my life these days -- winning at crime, losing at love.

Finally a cab stops for the valet's signal, I slip inside. "Santa Monica, please" I tell the driver. Maybe it's not too late for pizza delivery. I hate to cook, but I do like to eat.

My cell phone rings. I rummage through the jumble in my purse, laying my Glock out of the way on the seat as I search for it.

The driver looks nervously in his mirror at the gun.

"It's okay," I tell him. "I have a license for it."

He doesn't look reassured.

I finally locate my phone. It's my boss. The universe must be paying me back for lying to Jeff.

"The bank's in trouble," Morgan yells over my cell phone. "I need you here. Now."

The universe is definitely pissed.

"On my way," I say and disconnect. My life would be

much nicer if people didn't yell at me.

I can't imagine what's happened in the short time since I left. It must be concerning or he wouldn't be calling me. I'm Morgan's least favorite employee. Of course everything's a crisis with him. If he can't find his favorite pen, it's an emergency. Still, this might be serious.

I hang up and instruct the driver, "Change of plans. Take me two blocks over to the Bank of Beverly Hills."

The driver's eyes widen. He glances at my gun, then back to me.

"The bank?"

CHAPTER THREE

The cab stops in front of the bank. Or should I say pauses. As soon as both my feet hit the pavement, I'm almost blown over by turbulence as the cab driver floors the gas pedal and peels away. The screech of his tires is deafening.

Bud, the head of security, lets me in the front doors. Getting on in years, he still maintains his military bearing and a twinkle in his eyes.

"What's up with the boss?" I ask.

He shakes his head. "No idea. He went home like usual at closing. Then an hour ago he comes back all upset."

***

I exit the elevator on the bank's top floor and head directly for Morgan's office.

Inside, I find my boss seated with his head down on his desk. In his late fifties, Morgan normally reminds me of a bloodhound with the bags below his eyes and loose floppy

13

jowls. A recent diet has only exaggerated those features. As he lifts his head, I can see his face is such a deep, beet red. I immediately become alarmed. He looks as if he could have a stroke any minute.

"Are you all right? Should I call an ambulance?" I ask.

"Took you long enough to get here."

What? All of five minutes. "Let me call your wife."

"No, no, don't do that. Stop fussing. Lexi, it's three million dollars. Embezzled. Gone."

For real? Three million. This can't be good. "Wait," I say. "Take a deep breath and let me bring you a glass of water. Then you can tell me from the beginning."

I return from his private bathroom with the water to find he's still sitting in the same position, but now tears are rolling down his face. This is a Morgan I've never seen before. It's usually his employees who do all the crying.

He swallows the water and sets down the glass. "Lexi, this will ruin the bank."

"Shouldn't our Federal insurance cover embezzlement?"

He looks at me like I'm crazy. "The money's not the problem."

Seems like a problem to me.

"If the news leaks out, our clients won't be able to withdraw their money fast enough. It will be like that Wells Fargo debacle with the fraudulent accounts. I'll be a laughing stock."

14

I should have known. The tears are for himself. Still, he's definitely working himself into the hospital if I can't calm him down.

"What happened?" I ask.

"Mac Parker called."

I pause. That's a name everyone in the bank, and probably most people in the world, know well. Mac is a big movie star in his mid forties. He's popular, handsome, and all smiles to the public. In private, he's mean and tight-fisted to the people who work with or for him. Like us.

"He's coming back early next week from a four month shoot in Spain and discovered that his new office manager, Willis Creiger, cleaned out all the money from his operating account. Over three million dollars. He's threatening to sue us."

"Didn't Mac sign papers to give Willis access to his accounts?"

He nods.

"Then there's no malfeasance on the part of the bank. We weren't robbed. He was."

Morgan shakes his head. "I told him that. He says he doesn't care, he'll ruin us if we don't replace it. He's claiming negligence on our part. It's a public relations disaster. Everyone in town will withdraw their accounts if they think it's unsafe here."

Morgan's right. Most people won't question Mac's lies if he tells them that it's our fault. Even though Beverly

Hills is a famous place, and we have other well known clients, this is a small privately owned bank, without the resources of the big international chains I've worked for before. He could start a run on the bank. I doubt if the bank will go under, but we would definitely take a severe hit in loss of clients.

"Still," I repeat, "Not our problem. It's Mac's."

"He says if we haven't replaced the money by the time he's back, he's going to file charges against us," Morgan says. "It's a catastrophe. The media will be all over us."

Not good. In the end, the courts would side with us. But the bank will be dragged through months or even years of legal battles that could easily cost more than the three million that was stolen. And our federal insurance won't cover us because it's Mac's money that was stolen.

I can picture Mac's face on every morning and late night talk show. He's a good enough actor that he can persuade viewers that he's the victim and generate tons of bad publicity for the bank. There's not a news or entertainment show in existence that wouldn't happily give him airtime.

Morgan runs his hands through his hair. "You're the hot shot fraud investigator. Do something."

"Of course," I agree in an effort to make him relax. "Let me go check out Mac's account and his thieving manager."

"I wish Howard was here. He'd know how to take care

of this."

I wish he was here, too. Howard's head of the fraud department and my immediate boss. Unfortunately he's on vacation in Kenya with his son, leaving me in charge.

"Maybe I can track the money. You should lie down. Try to rest."

"Lexi, if we lose customers, I might have to close the bank."

That stuns me.

The job market is terrible at the moment. A closure would throw most of the employees under a bus, even if they eventually manage to be re-hired elsewhere. They have mortgages, babies, family medical needs, kids in college, debt... That's not right.

Wow. This is the night that keeps on giving. If the bank comes under censure, and with my history with the police, I can forget ever having another job in fraud investigation. I can't imagine being totally barred from chasing white collar thieves. I understand ninety-eight percent of employees hate their jobs, but I'm one of the few who loves what I do.

I force down my worry and vow to myself that I'll locate the money, even if I have to catch this employee of Mac's myself.

"We can talk about that later," I manage. "Get some rest."

Back in my own office, I slip off my good work heels and slide my feet into my comfy crocodile slippers. I take a quick glance around the room.

Being a workaholic, I spend most of my time here, I've rearranged things to suit myself. I've replaced the bank's boring landscape prints with eight by ten photos of local and international con men and criminals. About half have red marker "Xs" scrawled across their faces. Those are my favorites. They're the ones whose careers I've ended.

Having worked here for a couple years, I figured things were going to be okay work wise. Last month, I even invested in my first house. It's being rehabbed at the moment. If Morgan fires me, I'll never even get to move into it. Any loss of income is a disaster because I'm totally stretched financially.

I head to my desk, ignoring the pile of discarded clothes on the couch, the dirty mugs, and last night's empty take out cartons on the file cabinet. If I get fired, someone else can deal with them. I figured out a long time ago that when life is over, there is no prize for neatness.

Once signed into my computer, it doesn't take long to see that Willis arranged two days ago to wire three million dollars of Mac's money to a Cayman Island account. Not good. Cayman Island banks aren't known for being helpful.

To follow this money trail, see if any of it's recoverable, and do a complete background check on this guy Willis quickly, I'm going to need help.

I punch in Steve Harrison's number. Morgan didn't say I couldn't call his son. Fresh out of college and over my vehement protests, Steve was assigned to me as a trainee. I think Morgan did it to piss me off, but Howard sees promise in the boy.

I try hard not to hold the fact against Steve that he's related to Morgan. Or the fact that he's twenty-two, rich, charming, and attractive. Obviously, he's nothing like his father, except for the rich part.

Steve answers his phone instantly, "Hey, Lexi, what's up?"

"Look, I hate to bother you, but we have a problem here. Can you come in to the office?"

"Now? Can't it wait 'til tomorrow? I'm with a date at the Dodgers game."

It must be with one of those women who doesn't mind that Steve's rich, charming, and attractive. I've heard there are women who go for that sort of thing in a man.

"This is important. Your dad may need you and I definitely do."

"Dad's there this late? What's going on?"

"I'll tell you as soon as you're here."

"Tell me now."

"Not on the phone."

"That bad? I'm on my way." He hangs up.

CHAPTER FOUR

Steve arrives forty-five minutes later, still wearing his Dodger's cap.

"I stopped by Dad's office. He doesn't look good," he says. "Mom's coming to pick him up. What's happened? He told me to help you, but no details."

I explain about Mac and his threats.

"This is bad," he says when I finish. "No wonder Dad's freaked out. Mac's a first class jerk."

"Sorry about interrupting your night out."

"It's okay. She was kind of clingy anyway. Ever hear again from that crooked boyfriend of yours? Andre. The one that landed you in jail?"

"Not a word in over a year. And he's not my boyfriend. If I knew where he was, I'd report him to Interpol."

***

The sun's rising the next morning by the time we give up trying to track the money. It was forwarded too many

license, no work records. Either he's an identity thief or in witness protection. Hopefully, we can learn more at his place.

"This is cool," Steve says. "Here we are out cruising for bad guys again. Like in Sumatra last year. We're exactly like Rizzoli and Isles, Castle and Becket, Sherlock and Watson - -"

"-- Abbot and Costello?"

"Come on, I'm serious."

"We aren't looking for bad guys. We're looking for one guy in order to trace Mac's money."

"Bet you find bad guys plural. You always do. Like Javier and his father last year in Sumatra."

I shake my head.

"Come on. How about that stock manipulator you exposed in Tokyo who was pretending to be a bank executive? He had two other people helping him. Or the time you figured out that a client sold her valuable jewelry through friends and then claimed it was stolen from her bank box. You found her jewelry with a dealer in Budapest."

"What? Have you researched all the cases I ever worked on?"

"Maybe a few of them."

His cell rings. "Hi, Skylar," he says. "Sorry I had to end our date early last night....No, today's not good for me. I'm working...Look, I'll need to call you back. This isn't a good time. Bye."

Minutes later, we arrive at Willis' house. It's a nice place located on a shady street halfway down the north side of the hill between Mulholland Drive and Ventura Boulevard. The neighborhood is an older, quiet one with lots of flowers and trees.

The view from the front of Willis' small stucco house is a spectacular one of the San Fernando Valley below.

I park my vintage 1990 silver Supra behind a red Mustang in front of Willis' house.

"Let's hope that's his car. Maybe he's still here," I say. "How lucky is that."

We get out and pass through a low hedge to reach Willis' front door. As we do, I notice a curtain twitch at the house next door. A middle-aged woman peeks out at us. Nosy neighbors are probably the second best security you can have. Dogs are the first, of course. And the one I can hear inside Willis' house is barking up a storm. It sounds like a smallish dog from the timber of its voice.

Steve rings the doorbell. The dog inside turns frantic. There's a narrow, deeply tinted bronze glass panel beside the door. In the dark interior, I can barely make out what appears to be a mixed-breed Westie. I say mixed-breed because it has spots all over it and West Highland Terriers, Westies for short, are normally solid white. This one scratches wildly at the door.

I regard the dog as a good sign. Willis must still be

around. No dog person would leave their dog locked inside and take off. Still, no one responds to the bell.

Steve rings again with the same result.

"There's a woman home at the place next door. See if she knows anything," I say. "I'm going to walk around back."

Steve heads over there, and I let myself through the side gate into the fenced back yard. The yard is beautiful with tall hedges of pink bougainvillea down both sides. A low fence marks the far end of the mowed area. Beyond the fence is a dirt lane that parallels the street in front.

Orange and lemon trees give the yard a warm, inviting look. All together, the yard is breathtakingly beautiful. There's even a small vegetable garden with tomatoes, beans, and peppers. If I lived here, I'd spend all my time out in this yard. Too bad Willis stole money from Mac. Otherwise, I'd employ him in a heartbeat to landscape my new house. Maybe he has a gardener. I'll have to get his name from Willis before I arrest him.

I walk carefully along the flagstone path in an effort to keep my good work heels from being ruined by sinking into the dirt.

I approach the back door and peer inside. The dog unexpectedly leaps up on the other side of the glass and gives me a fright. I hastily take a step back. Then I look again at the dog through the clear, sunlit glass of the back door.

I draw my Glock. Those aren't spots on the dog's coat, it's blood. And it doesn't look like the dog is injured.

I try the rear door. It's unlocked. Never a good sign. I open it cautiously. As I hoped, the dog charges out into the yard. Before he can reverse to reach me, I slip in and close the door, leaving him outside, still barking.

I find myself in a dimly lit kitchen. By the sink is a dog's water bowl with the name Frosty on it.

I resist the urge to call out Willis' name until I can figure out what's going on.

There are bloody paw prints everywhere. Silently I search the first floor rooms. Nothing appears out of place in the dining room or the living room. I head down the hallway, quietly checking closets and the bathroom as I go. The back room on the first floor appears to be a home office with a computer, books, and other electronics. It looks neat and well organized.

I return to the hall and head up the stairs. I go slowly through the guest bedroom and then move cautiously on to the master. The bloody paw prints are all over the place.

I move quietly into the master bedroom doorway and pause. Even though the room is dark with all the curtains pulled closed, there's enough light to see it's been trashed. Lamps knocked over, an upholstered wing chair on its side, and smashed bric-a-brac. A suitcase has its contents strewn across the floor with its lining ripped out.

Near the bed is a man I recognize from the bank's

security footage as Willis. He lies on his face with a deep gash in the side of his head. I kneel to feel for a pulse, even though I already know from looking at him that it's too late. There isn't one. Of all the things I hoped to find here, his body wasn't one of them.

I dial nine-one-one as I stand to make a quick check of the master bath. It's clear, but, as I pass the mirror, I notice there are blood stains on my clothes.

Still waiting for nine-one-one to answer, I grasp the door handle of the walk-in closet to look inside.

Wham! The door explodes in my face. I fly backwards, going down hard. My head bangs hard against the floor. My gun skitters away.

Someone dashes past me. I scramble to my feet, slipping badly and going down again as the emergency operator finally answers, "Nine-one-one. What's your emergency?"

"Help. Murder." I yell into the phone as I race in pursuit.

The back door opens and slams shut while I'm still on the stairs. By the time I arrive in the back yard, Frosty's barking fiercely.

I charge toward the back fence, but my heels sink in the dirt. I pause to kick them off. Rushing to the fence, I look up and down the lane. Too late. The intruder is gone.

Over Frosty's barking, I can hear the voice of the nine-one-one operator frantically trying to get my attention.

My frustration boils over. I almost had him, but he managed to escape. And I'll bet the key to locating the missing three million dollars went with him.

CHAPTER FIVE

I stroke Frosty in an effort to calm him as we wait for the police to arrive. Poor dog. He's really upset. I can't blame him. I am, too. If only I'd been more careful, I could have caught the killer.

Steve approaches. "The neighbor says the dog's been barking like crazy since early this morning."

I slip my Glock and my car keys into his pocket. "Do me a favor. Lock that under the seat in my car. The police don't need to know I have a gun with me." While he takes care of the gun, I step across the yard to the neighbor's to see if she'll take care of Frosty until Willis' relatives can arrive and take possession. I love dogs, but I'm not home enough to have one of my own. He's a sweet dog. It's worth the money I offer her to be sure he's taken care of.

***

Four hours later, I'm sitting in an interrogation room, waiting to be interviewed. I'm shivering in the worn cotton jump suit they gave me when my dress was confiscated as evidence, along with my ruined shoes. I wasn't even allowed to go in the bathroom and wash up, until the police technicians took scrapings and pictures of me from all angles. Losing the clothes doesn't really matter as I can't imagine ever wearing them again.

Being in a police interview room brings a host of horrific memories pouring back from the case that almost sent me to prison. It was a terrifying experience.

A couple years ago in Australia, I was held as a possible accomplice in the theft of a Rembrandt. Something I knew nothing about. The Australian police finally let me go, but the incident cost me my job in New York and my reputation. Banks aren't keen on employing fraud investigators who have been suspected of theft. It's also the reason Morgan and a few of the employees don't like me.

Even worse, the painting was actually stolen by notorious Andre Van der Meer, a man I innocently loved and thought I had married. When our marriage turned out to be a scam, I should have been relieved. Especially when I learned the truth of Andre's identity, but I wasn't. I wish I knew if the love was a sham, too.

He and the painting disappeared after that. I never saw him again until last year in Sumatra. Stupid me, I let him right back into my heart. And then he strolled right out again. I'm great at my job, but I sure suck at relationships.

My fingers involuntarily touch the antique silver cross

necklace I always wear. As soon as I realize what I'm doing, I remove my hand. The cross was a gift from Andre before things went sour.

I put Andre out of my head and try to relax. Steve must be in another room nearby. If I hadn't been covered in blood with a developing black eye from being hit by the closet door, we might have been able to just give our statements to the police at Willis' house.

No sleep, a pounding headache, and crashing adrenalin are all taking a toll on me. I'm definitely not at my best.

The interrogation room door opens and the lead detective from Willis' place, a tall, lean Latina woman in her late thirties who has a "seen it all expression" enters. She's followed by her partner, a restless, wiry black man in his forties. She sits opposite me as he takes a position leaning against the wall.

"Miss Winslow," says the woman. "I'm Detective Lupita Jovar and this is Detective Calvin Farrell. We'd like to hear your version of the events this morning."

I nod that that's fine, "This is being recorded, right?"

"Of course," comes from Farrell. "I'm sure with your history, you remember how this works."

Uh, oh. These guys did do their homework. "I was never charged with anything."

"Yeah," he says. "I read the report. For lack of evidence, it said. That doesn't mean you weren't guilty, only that the Australian police couldn't prove it."

That's exactly what everyone else thought, too. Including my former employers who immediately fired me.

I take a deep breath before explaining step-by-step what happened this morning. I add that we were notified of account irregularities by Mac, but not the amount. We were at Willis' to follow up since he's -- was -- Mac's manager.

"What were these burning irregularities that brought you to Willis' house at such an early in hour of the morning?" he asks.

"That's confidential bank business." My go to excuse for not giving details.

Jovar doesn't like my answer. Farrell scowls.

"How was Willis killed?" I ask.

Jovar cuts me off. "Why did you enter the premises?"

"I saw blood on the dog. I didn't know if Willis was hurt and needed help.""How did you get in?"

"As I said at the house, the back door was open."

"You made a mess of the crime scene. Your fingerprints are on almost all the doors inside the house. Why is that?" Farrell asks as he starts pacing.

"I didn't know where he was."

"You thought he might be hiding in a closet?"

"Somebody certainly was."

They're not liking that answer either, but at least it's the truth.

"Did you find any fingerprints on the inside of the bedroom closet door?" I ask.

They ignore me again. "Were you expecting trouble?" Jovar asks.

"Not until I saw the blood all over the dog."

"Did you know Willis well?"

"I don't...didn't know him."

"Why's his blood all over you?"

The interview repetition continues for another half hour.

I feel terrible that I can't help with a description of the person in the closet. The room was too dark and he was too fast. I have absolutely nothing to give the police. It's obvious they don't trust me. Mad as I was at Willis, he didn't deserve what happened. I wanted to ask them if they learned Willis' real name, but I couldn't ask without revealing that we had researched him.

In the end, Jovar and Farrell reluctantly let us go. They're suspicious, even though the neighbor corroborated our arrival time. It was even obvious to me that Willis had been dead for a while before we got there. Thank goodness for observant neighbors.

CHAPTER SIX

Steve and I return to the bank, Steve takes a break on my office couch to watch the news on the internet. After I step into my office bathroom where I keep a change of clothes for emergencies, we continue working.

Finally frustrated with my lack of success researching Willis, I hurl my pen at the far wall.

Steve watches me. "Feel better?"

"Not even close."

Morgan called Mac earlier about Willis' death and got Mac to give us longer to find his money before filing charges. I'd like to tell Mac to go ahead and do his worst, but that's me. I twist my mind back to Willis.

"Willis has no job history, no social media, and no family. Why on earth did Mac hire this guy?"

"Too bad we don't have his fingerprints," Steve says.

"Of course, but the police aren't going to share. Maybe

they had luck with the next-door neighbor. Or located some family information at Willis' house."

I think about the problem a little longer. "How would anyone know Willis had the three million unless he told them? A sum that large probably wouldn't be available for immediate withdrawal either. It could still be sitting in a bank somewhere."

"Maybe the killer made him write a check for it and he's at a bank right now arranging to cash it. Or the money is already gone," says Steve.

"That's a bad thought."

"Or the murderer already has it."

"Then he would have had no reason to still be at Willis' when we got there."

"Unless we arrived before he could leave?"

"Willis had already been dead for several hours before we arrived..."

We share a moment of silence.

"Seems most likely Willis was killed for the money," Steve says. "The timing would be too coincidental to be anything else."

He looks at me, suddenly alert. "Do you think the police found the money?"

"They didn't let anything slip to that effect."

"Could there be a link to the money at the house?"

"Possible..."

"If the police found either the money or its location,

shouldn't the bank claim it?"

"Definitely, if we were sure they have it. Otherwise we're alerting them to the fact that it's missing."

"Yeah, dad wouldn't like that."

He would not. I also don't like his father's constant desire to hide information from the police, either. It cuts us off from a major resource.

I'm mulling my annoyance over when we notice the last story on the news. It's a short bit about Willis. Very short. As in "Local man, Willis Creiger, dies in a home accident" short. "Mr. Creiger worked as office manager for international movie star Mac Parker. Parker was unavailable for comment."

Unbelievable. Home accident, my ass. Who do the police think was hiding in his closet? The tooth fairy? Do they think I lied about it? Maybe Jovar and Farrell aren't as smart as I gave them credit for. There's only one thing left to do.

Steve stares at me. "You're thinking of going back to Willis' place aren't you?"

I don't answer.

"It'll be faster with two," he says.

Drat. I'm going to have to be more careful. The kid is starting to read my mind.

CHAPTER SEVEN

The sun is barely peeking over the horizon. Steve and I, dressed in jogging outfits, sprint up the dirt lane behind Willis' house. My sandy blonde hair is tucked up under a Lakers' baseball cap. An over-sized pair of sunglasses covers my black eye and most of my face. I'm wearing an empty backpack. Steve has his Dodgers cap pulled low over his forehead and aviator style reflective sunglasses. We pause at Willis' back fence. pretending to stretch.

"I still think we should have come last night," Steve whispers.

"I told you, there's nothing like seeing flashlights in a dark empty house to make the neighbors speed dial nine-one-one. Much better that we've come after the sun is up. Still, we'll need to be fast and leave before the police or the crime scene cleaners show up."

We watch and listen. No one is around. Even better, there's no barking. I check the backyard. It's exactly as I'd remembered. The shrubbery and fence will hide our arrival from the prying eyes of all the nearby neighbors.

We exchange nods, hop the fence, and dash across Willis' yard. We pause at the back door to look and listen again. No sign of Frosty or any watchful eyes.

Steve acts as look-out while we pull on latex gloves. I lift the yellow police tape and insert my lock picks into the door. Uh, oh. The door isn't locked. Just like yesterday. That's pretty careless of the police to leave it open. I slowly turn the handle and motion for Steve to follow silently. Inside, I close the door behind us, leaving it unlocked and look around.

If Willis' bedroom was a mess yesterday, now the kitchen matches the destruction. Grimy fingerprint dust covers every surface. The counters are littered with dirty coffee cups and remains of fast food take-out wrappings. Frosty's water bowl is tipped over. There's been no attempt to wipe up the spill. Packages from the freezer are ripped open. Cereal boxes are strewn about.

I put my finger to my lips to silence Steve. I point out the freezer packages and dumped food. "Not the police," I whisper.

Silently I head toward Willis' office on the first floor. Steve follows close behind.

We pause in the doorway in shock. The desk drawers gape open crookedly with all the files and every piece of paper dumped in the center of the room, exactly like the kitchen.

The police were probably responsible for most of the filthy kitchen, but, like the freezer packages, they didn't do this either. There are clean papers lying on top of those with fingerprint powder. Someone has been here since the police left.

The murderer must not have found what they wanted yesterday, and like us, returned.

Steve's eyes widen as I pull my gun. I signal him again for silence. What if the intruder is still here? Good. I'd love another crack at the jerk who slammed the closet door in my face.

Steve doesn't carry a gun, so he picks up a heavy bookend from the desk. That makes me smile as I remember how our first case together in Sumatra got ugly at one point, turning into a nasty free-for-all. Steve swung a mean desk lamp to good effect. We move quietly from room to room carefully, opening any closed closets with extreme caution.

However, most of the closet doors are already yawning open with their contents pulled out and dumped on the floor. Unfortunately, the perpetrator appears to be long gone. Maybe if we'd come last night like Steve wanted, we would have caught them.

Steve and I have a hushed discussion when we finish checking the house. We decide he'll return to Willis' office and pick his way through the trashed files. I'll scope out the other rooms.

"Hmm," whispers Steve. "Do you think Willis worked from home or has an office elsewhere?"

"Even if he used another office, he probably worked from home while Mac is out of town. I don't think Willis would have kept anything personal there, either.

"What we really need is his computer," says Steve.

"I expect the police have it. I don't expect they'll be likely to share. Collect anything here you find regarding Willis' financial matters, personal history, contacts, and put them in my backpack. We'll read them later."

There's a pencil jar on the desk. Funny how often people stuff odd things in their pencil jars. On a hunch, I tip it over. The usual paper clips, coins, a couple pretty rocks, and a staple remover tumble out. Nothing useful. A key falls out of the very bottom. It's marked with a galloping horse. It must be a spare for the Mustang parked in front. I hope the police checked it over. No way will Steve or I be able to search it, much as I'd like to. It's too visible to the neighbors.

I head upstairs to check out the bedroom. After an hour, I start feeling nervous that we've been here too long. I stand and stretch my stiff back. I can't shake the feeling we're wasting our time. I know I certainly wouldn't relish another go-round with Jovar and Farrell if we're caught here.

I head back to the office where Steve has amassed a

small pile of documents. "Five more minutes and we're leaving. Finish up while I take another walk around," I tell him.

I pause in the living room and notice the floor to ceiling bookcase that had been crammed with books and bric-a-brac yesterday. Now the contents are all tossed on the floor. Another thing I don't think the police did.

Curious as to Willis' reading choices, I pick through a few books and read the titles. There are several on gardening, a few about geology, and one on puppy care with a photo of Frosty tucked inside. Hmm. Maybe someone was looking for something that might be secreted inside a book. That's an easy place to tuck a note or a bank account code.

I start flipping the books open as I pick them up. I'm having no luck until I open a worn copy of Stingaree by E.W. Hornung. Inside, there's an inscription that reads -- Happy Birthday, Ted.

Probably a used or borrowed book. The next title is a Ned Kelly biography. If I remember right, Stingaree and Ned Kelly were both bank robbers - one fictional, one real. Interesting reading choices for someone who also robbed a bank.

I open the Ned Kelly book and inside there's an old photograph that looks like it might be of a younger Willis with an attractive woman of about the same age. In the picture, they're standing against a building wall.

Unfortunately there's no indication of what building or where it's located. I turn the picture over, but there's no inscription on the back.

"Steve," I call. "I wonder if the killer found what he was looking for this time?"

Steve appears in the doorway with a huge smile. He's waving a thick manila envelope.

"Not if he was looking for this. It was stuffed inside the cushion of the office chair. I didn't notice it until I sat on it."

I flip through the envelope. There's an airplane ticket, and other official looking documents.

"Way to go! Looks like you hit the jackpot." I could kiss him, but he might take it the wrong way. But he definitely wins a gold star.

As I show him the photo I found, I realize something odd about Willis' house. "What's missing in this house?" I ask Steve.

He shakes his head.

"There aren't any family pictures or ones of him with anyone except this one from inside a book. No photographs at all. It adds to the idea he's hiding something."

"That is weird," he says. "Should we look in all the books?"

I look at the large number of books on the floor. "There's not enough time to do a truly good search. We're pushing our luck staying here this long already."

We agree to another fifteen minutes max. Just then car doors slam outside. A peek out the window confirms our time's up. Drat. The crime scene cleaners are here. "Let's go," I say. "Got the backpack?"

He nods.

In a flash, we're out the back door and down the dirt lane.

CHAPTER EIGHT

I clear the trash from earlier food deliveries cluttering my office table. Steve spreads out the papers from Willis' place.

I open the plane ticket first. It's in Willis' name traveling to Adelaide, Australia dated for today. Steve and I exchange a stunned look. Willis was leaving the country. If he'd left one day earlier, he might still be alive.

Next are Willis' rental agreements for his Studio City house and for his Mustang. He was behind in payments for both.

Then things get more interesting.

We find a life insurance policy for two hundred thousand dollars in the name of Ted Collins with the proceeds payable to a Joan Lassiter and then Emily Lassiter.

"I saw where Willis sent money to a credit card in the

name of Joan Lassiter," Steve says.

We mull that over, but we don't have enough information to know who Ted, Joan, and Emily are to Willis.

Steve hands me what appears to be a deed for a property in Coober Pedy, South Australia, also in the name of the Lassiters. Stapled to the deed are a couple other legal looking documents titled license and lease.

I mention the book inscription "To Ted from Mom" inside the cover. Ted Collins must be a close friend or maybe a relative."

"What now?" he asks.

"At least we have more names to follow up."

"Shouldn't we tell the police what we found and that someone searched the house after they left?"

"First we'd have to explain how we know that."

"Oh," he says. "I don't like lying to the authorities."

That makes two of us.

"Why don't you go over Willis' bank accounts. See what he did with his money. Maybe how he spent it will give us a clue."

After a bit, I stretch my arms over my head. I decide to head for the break room. I'm in serious need of caffeine.

I pass two of the tellers returning from a break. I nod politely, but they both pretend not to notice. I hear them whispering after I pass. It hurts, but it's nothing new. They're among the ones that think I'm guilty for the theft of the Rembrandt and shouldn't be allowed to work here.

Steve joins me in the break room. We decide to discuss what we've learned so far. I start. "I changed my research to Australia and still can't find any mention of a Willis Creiger. I'm wondering about his connection to Ted Collins and the Lassiters."

"Wait until you see Willis' financial records," says Steve, "Best I can make out from them is that every penny he earned for the past year few years was sent to a credit card in the name of Joan Lassiter. I tried a search on her name, too, but there are a gadzillion Joan Lassiters. Same with Emily Lassiter and Ted Collins. Too many to pick the right one with the information we have so far."

"See if the credit card company will give you an address for the Lassiters without a warrant. And ask if there was a recent deposit of three million dollars. I'll work on Ted Collins next."

Steve's cell rings. He answers and talks for a minute while I make a new pot of coffee. As I do, I notice that I've managed to drip parts of my breakfast down the front of my new blouse. Rats. I don't have a top in my closet that doesn't have a food stain somewhere. At least I finally got smart and no longer support my local cleaner. I redid my closet. My tops are now all washable prints in dark colors. I still spill things, but at least the spots aren't as visible now.

Steve ends his call. He takes one look at my blouse, wets a paper towel, and hands it to me without comment.

I thank him and dab the wet towel over the spots.

"That was Dad. He says his doctor wants him to come to the hospital for a few tests."

"He's okay?" I ask.

"He says he is. They're only double-checking."

Good, that will keep Morgan out of my hair for a few days.

Steve adds, "He also said for us to leave no stone unturned."

On a hunch, I dial the police department and ask when Willis' body will be released by the morgue.

Their answer stuns me. Apparently the body has already been claimed by his sister. That was fast. The police won't say anything else. Not even her name.

I sit down abruptly in the nearest chair and repeat for Steve what the police said. Questions race through my head. A sister? The police must have found an address book or contacts in Willis' computer. Could Joan and Emily Lassiter be his sisters?

The police must really think Willis died because of an accident. Am I wrong? No way they'd release the body that fast otherwise. Would I think it was a murder if someone hadn't been hiding in the closet? Or if I didn't know about the money? Maybe not.

Steve listens as I quickly call the morgue in the Valley. I explain to the receptionist that I'm a friend of Willis' and I would like to know what mortuary the body is being released to. She tells me it's the Daughtry Brothers Crematorium and Mortuary. The body is scheduled for release tomorrow morning.

I punch four-one-one again for the number to Daughtry Brothers. A man informs me that there will be no funeral. The body is to be embalmed immediately upon arrival. They also refuse to share the sister's name, citing her request for privacy.

I tell Steve, "We don't know if this woman claiming the body is really his sister. I think our best chance of finding the money is figuring out who killed him. Normally we'd follow the money. But since that's not possible here, we better follow the body."

CHAPTER NINE

With Los Angeles' morning rush hour in full swing on the nearby streets, I sit in Steve's BMW. We're parked with a clear view of the both entrance and the side loading area of the Daughtry Brothers Crematorium and Mortuary. The binoculars in my lap are good enough that if anyone in the parking lot smiles widely enough, I can probably count the fillings in their back molars.

Seconds later, Steve slides into the driver's seat with a bag of breakfast biscuits and coffee from a place down the block.

"The body arrive yet?" He asks

I shake my head and take a bite.

Steve's cell rings. "Hello...Hey Skylar...No, I'm not ducking you...Yes, I meant to call...but I'm working. Listen, why don't I call you back tonight?...No, I won't forget. Bye."

"Skylar your current girlfriend?"

"No. The ball game the other night was our first date."

"You were right, she does seem clingy."

*****

Breakfast is a distant memory, as is lunch by the time the mortuary van arrives. We wait until the driver backs up to the loading dock.

"Let me do the office," Steve asks.

I nod. Since we've watched only one employee, a young woman, unlock and enter the building since we arrived, Steve might have better luck with getting answers than I would. His charm does have uses.

An hour later, the mortuary van is long gone. I'm totally bored. Steve's still in the morgue. My only excitement is letting a call from Jeff roll over into my voicemail.

Another twenty minutes go by and I'm thinking Steve shouldn't be taking this long. I hope he's not spending his time chit-chatting with the young woman because she's cute. Maybe I'd better go in and drag him out.

I'm relieved when I finally spot him racing back to the car. But why is he running...?

He practically rips his car door off in his hurry to hop in.

"Lexi, Willis' body is being shipped to Australia tonight."

Australia? I've been praying the case wasn't going there.

Nausea rises in my throat and I can feel the blood drain from my face.

"I can't go there ."

"I know. You were arrested. But that's in the past. You were never charged."

"Not because they didn't want to. One Detective Inspector even swore he'd arrest me if I ever set foot in Sydney again."

"Then we're good. The casket is headed for Adelaide. That's almost nine hundred miles west of Sydney."

That's not far enough for me. "You go," I say. "It can be your first solo trip."

Steve smiles. "You really think I'm ready?"

"Sure," I lie. "Since it's the only option. I'm not going."

"How's that guy even going to know you're there? We'll be in and out. Come on. We have to be at the airport tonight if we're going on the same flight as the casket."

My hands are trembling. I wish they wouldn't do that whenever I'm stressed. It's like having a 'tell' while you're playing poker.

I can't reveal to Steve that his father threatened my job if I don't recover the money. He's not responsible for his father's callousness.

I don't answer.

"Well, I'm going even if I have to go alone," Steve says. "There are too many people at the bank that need their jobs."

Interesting, we both feel that way. I know that one of the tellers is working two jobs to pay off college debt. Bud, the head of security, has a special needs child that drains his income already. Eleanor, an assistant in human resources, is trying to save enough money to move out of her mother's basement. Losing our paychecks, even for a short time, could cause a lot of pain for everyone.

Steve interrupts my thoughts. "Look, you're the one who said we need to follow the body."

I ignore him and continue thinking. There's not much choice for me here. Let the other employees down, forfeit my new house, lose my job and never have another one in my field, or risk being arrested in Australia. Talk about a rock and a hard place. Why does my life come down to these kinds of choices? I can't envision my future if I'm not a fraud investigator. Of course making license plates in an Australian prison doesn't have a lot of appeal either.

Neither of us says another word as we return to my office.

"Okay," I manage to say. "I'll go."

"Really? What changed your mind?"

"Don't ask questions."

"Great. You're the best."

I give him a dirty look. There's nothing great about it. "You know our chances of finding the money are miniscule at best."

"You can do it."

Good grief. He actually means it.

Three hours later, after a frantic dash through the bank to grab my passport, order tickets, and apply online for visas, we're at LAX in a gift store, hoping desperately that approval for our visas comes through before our flight boards. We scramble to buy backpacks, tooth paste, brushes, shirts and pants. I add an electrical outlet converter. Steve grabs a travel guide.

We finish checkout, head to the flight's crowded waiting area, and find seats. Steve makes several calls to alert people he'll be out of the country. I realize sadly that no one cares where I am. My younger sister lives in Florida and calls me a jet-setter in a nasty way, even as I explain it's for work. If she ever went anywhere, she'd know flying these days isn't much fun. The only thing she wants from me is the checks I send for our mother who lives with her. My mother isn't interested in anything except her country club membership and maintaining her image with her society friends. They both make me feel like an outsider in my own family. It was my dad I was close to.

The next hour crawls by with no notice of our visa clearance. Without a visa, we won't be allowed on the plane. No visa, no plane trip, no job.

Steve drops the newspaper he's been reading. "Why'd you choose to work in fraud?"

"My dad was a diplomat. He died unexpectedly in Argentina, the summer before I went to college. He'd left a college fund for my sister and me. Plus there was a comfortable amount for my mother to live on and be independent if she was careful. While I was away at school freshman year, a man scammed my mother into investing in bogus oil stocks. Then he disappeared, taking all of our money. We went from being comfortable to being broke. I understand the desperation fraud causes to people's lives. That's when I learned the police consider fraud a crime against property and they have their hands full with crimes against people which is their first priority. So frauds fall between the cracks."

"Was the guy ever caught?"

"Took me two years. I finally tracked him down in Bismarck, North Dakota. He was trying to sell more bogus oil shares to another woman who was recently widowed. Big mistake. Turned out that the widow was the mother of the local sheriff. He and I had a short conversation. He was a nice guy with a very hot temper. He was so furious about his mother being conned, that the bogus stock guy may never get out of jail." I smile. It still makes me feel good to remember that day.

The loud speaker system blares "Boarding for Flight 62 to Melbourne and Adelaide. Please present your passports and visas with your ticket."

That's it then. We're not going to make this flight. It was our only shot. If we take a later one, it would be impossible to learn what happened to Willis' body.

Steve and I watch dejectedly as the other passengers file one-by-one through the gate. The line dwindles to zero.

"There goes our last lead," I say. Probably just as well. It was a crazy idea to follow Willis' body anyway.

The gate attendants call our names over the speakers with the words "last call" attached.

Suddenly my phone and Steve's ring simultaneously. It's the visa authorizations.

"Wait," I yell at the startled gate assistant who's closing the ramp door. "We're coming."

CHAPTER TEN

I stagger stiffly off the plane in Adelaide with a sun hat, oversized sunglasses, and cotton in my cheeks in an effort to fool the facial recognition of the airport cameras. I did the same thing when making our connection in Melbourne. Now my brain and my butt are equally numb. We passed customs in Melbourne. For me, it was an anxious time thinking the police might show up any minute to arrest me.

Steve waits at the head of the ramp for me. Our tickets were last minute so we couldn't get seats next to each other.

As I reach him, he points excitedly out the window to where the baggage-handlers unload our plane's luggage. A hearse waits nearby on the tarmac. It must be for Willis' casket. Its door bears a sign saying Coober Pedy Mortuary.

"Rats," I say.

"Why? What's Coober Pedy?" He asks.

"A town at least nine hours away -- in the outback."

"We better hurry to the car rental."

"No way in a car. The Stuart Highway that goes to Coober Pedy is infamous. If you aren't in a casket when you start the trip, you could be before you arrived there. Getting a bus would take too long. We need a plane."

We pause near a long row of poster-sized ads. Maybe a car is our only choice, I think.

"Look, Lexi," says Steve.

I look where he's pointing. There's a tour guide greeting people deplaning from our flight with a sign that says "Coober Pedy Charter Tours." I nod and he hurries over to speak with her. I cross my fingers. The tour guide listens and nods at Steve. Moments later, he's writing a check. That's a good sign.

He beckons me as she gathers a small group around her.

"We leave in fifteen minutes," he says. "They had two cancellations and if we wanted to pay for the whole tour package, we were welcome to the seats. We're booked as Mr. and Mrs. Harrison. I just had to show my driver's license.

Steve did well. Very well. Minus the Mr. and Mrs. bit.

Shortly, and under serious protest from my body, we're in puddle jumper of a charter plane headed to Coober Pedy. Not that there's any water below after the halfway mark. It's all a red sand and rocky desert interspersed with some scrub brush. I take off my sunglasses and remove the cotton from my cheeks.

I love Australia. It's a great place. The open spaces, the brilliant sunlight, and the wonderful people. I let out a sigh and begin to relax.

We couldn't arrange seats together again. Apparently there's a big event in Coober Pedy this coming weekend.

The person next to me is a short, plump Canadian woman in her fifties, dressed in pearls and a dress as well as pantyhose. Her eyes twinkle. Her smile is engaging. She's the kind of woman you like immediately.

"Hi, I'm Penny," she says. "You poor dear, what happened to your face?"

I'd totally forgotten my black eye. "A door ran into it."

She shakes her head. "Really dear, if you don't want to tell me, you don't need to. Otherwise you should come up with a better excuse than that."

"Honestly, that's what happened." I put the sunglasses back on. I don't want to be that memorable to strangers.

She gives me a look that says she doesn't believe a word. "Whoever he is, believe me, he isn't worth it."

I turn and look out the window.

"That's the Stuart Highway down there that you're looking at," she says. "It runs north from Adelaide to Coober Pedy then on past Uluru Rock and through Alice Springs and ends up in Darwin on the northern coast. Have you been to Coober Pedy before?"

"No, this is my first time in the outback."

"Me, too. I'm meeting friends, and we're going to take a tour of the desert on camels. Can you imagine? Camels."

"It sounds like fun." I say while trying to picture her short, round body swaying on top of a camel's hump. I can't quite make the image work and have to smother a giggle. It might be fun to travel here for pleasure if I didn't have to worry about Detective Inspector Ian Brode trying to arrest me.

"I'm hoping to see all sorts of Australian animals," Penny continues. "Kangaroos, emus, dingoes and...and, well, lots of other animals. Are you here for the Coober Pedy Prospector's Festival?"

I shake my head.

"I hear it's not to be missed. There's supposed to be a parade with floats, all kinds of races, games, booths, re-enactments, prizes, and barbeque. The locals and visitors dress up in costumes from the early nineteen hundreds when opals were first discovered."

"That will be fun. I'm traveling with my bro-husband. We'll see what's available when we get there and play it by ear."

She frowns when I say husband.

"No, he didn't hit me," I say. "He's a nice guy."

She doesn't believe a word.

I glance around the cabin. It's full with twelve passengers. I'm surprised to see a man among them who was on our flight to Adelaide. He doesn't look like a happy tourist. In his late forties, he's hard to miss as he's huge, sports a full bushy beard, and has the sourest expression I've seen in years. His dark sun glasses draw my attention, I wonder what or who he's hiding from.

People wearing sunglasses in inappropriate places always attract my interest since I use them myself as camouflage. Most facial identification technology uses eye measurements, among other things. At least I can tell by his build that he's not D.I. Brode.

I finally give up trying to remember what it is about him. It's probably unimportant.

***

Penny and I say goodbye when we land. As she moves away, she says, "Consider calling a home for battered women. They can help you."

I'm still smiling as I put my hat on. There's no way I'm taking the sunglasses off again either. I don't want any more people remembering me because of my black eye. As I hurry to join Steve at the top of the exit ramp, I catch myself nervously looking around for D.I. Brode in case he's here, waiting for me. Which I know is paranoid. I take a deep breath and try to shake it off my nerves.

"You're right about the Stuart Highway being dangerous," he says. "My book says it's such a hazard with cattle, kangaroos, emus, sheep, and camels crossing the road that most rental car agencies prohibit nighttime driving on it. It's supposed to be very tedious and drivers often fall asleep. It was redone recently. And it has a nickname. It's called The Track."

"The plane was a smart choice. We're here hours before the hearse can arrive."

I wish my body thought it was a smart thing. It just plain hurts. I'm not looking forward to riding on more planes when we go home.

"Did you know Coober Pedy is considered the opal capital of the world?" Steve asks, reading from his book.

I nod, secretly vowing to steal and destroy his guidebook the first chance I get. Either that or I'll have to introduce him to Penny. I have to smile at a funny mental picture in my head of the two of them trading Coober Pedy facts while riding on camels.

"Seems they've had huge discoveries of oil and gold recently, too."

"Sounds like the perfect destination for land sharks," I say.

Steve isn't sure what I mean.

"Land sharks are scam artists and con men."

"Right. I forgot you call them that."

Before we pick up our car, I head for the airport's tiny gift shop. Steve follows me in.

I check with the sales lady. I'm in luck. She has what I need. An aisle away, I spot the bearded man from the plane. Is he following us? No, as I check out, he's still in the back of the shop. Must be my over active imagination.

Steve meets me at the counter as the sales lady hands me my bag of purchases. "Look what I found," he says. He holds up a boomerang marked 'authentic' and 'handmade.' Grasped in his other hand is a huge Swiss army knife with a gadzillion blades. "Perfect, right?"

I'm not sure perfect for what, but he always makes me smile. His mind seems to race from sophisticated and professional to that of a happy puppy, excited about new experiences and people. And who isn't charmed by a happy puppy?

He buys his items before we head to the car rental desk. Steve looks curiously at my large paper gift shop bag, but doesn't ask what I bought.

"G'day, mates, welcome to the outback," the rental agent greets us. "Lucky you called ahead from Adelaide. You got the last car on the lot."

Steve grins.

"What?" I ask.

"I've been dying to hear someone say that."

"Say what?"

Steve whispers, "G'day, mate."

The agent assures us our four-wheel-drive SUV is ready and gassed up.

"We'll need a map to Coober Pedy and directions to reach the Stuart Highway," I tell the agent. "And a recommendation of a hotel."

"Big doings in Coober Pedy this week with the

Prospector's Festival. You won't find many available rooms."

He kindly obliges with directions as we'll still have to drive forty miles to reach town. Steve calls the number he suggests to book some rooms.

I'm studying the map and I hear him say, "Sure, we'll take the single room with the king bed. That's for Mr. and Mrs. Steve Harrison. Two adults."

I step in front of him and shake my head.

He covers the receiver with his hand. "I'm just being consistent."

"No!"

"It's all they have. Everything in town is booked."

"Try another hotel." Steve can tell I'm serious.

He says into the phone, "Correct that. We'll take both rooms." He hangs up and gives me a grin. "Can't blame a guy for trying."

"You'd need to be at least ten years older first."

"It's okay if a woman is ten years younger. Why not a guy?"

It's an old argument between us. It's a fair question, but he stops talking when he catches my annoyed expression.

By the time we get in the car and familiarize ourselves with its controls, it's late and very, very dark. Really dark as only a desert area can be. No need for my sunglasses now. In addition, Coober Pedy turns out to be one of those places that rolls up the sidewalk at nine p.m. Few buildings show any lights.

"How are we going to be able to find the hearse?" Steve asks.

"We find a business with some lights that shine on the road from Adelaide."

We head to the intersection of the Stuart Highway and Hutchison Street. According to the map, Hutchison is the first turn off from the Stuart Highway into Coober Pedy. Whether the hearse turns here or goes further north before heading into town, the driver has to pass this intersection.

We stop the car at the intersection and look around. There are only a few buildings. Those that do exist have closed for the night.

"There," says Steve. He points to a shuttered convenience store with parking lot lights that shine dimly across the highway.

The store might be closed for the night or permanently, it's hard to tell. But it looks like a perfect place to wait.

I park the SUV where it faces the intersection. A huge truck pulling several trailers passes without slowing. We're so close to the highway, the air stream of the truck train, as they're called, rocks our SUV.

Passing vehicles are few and far between. Steve closes his eyes and drifts off to sleep. I don't wake him. It's only necessary for one of us to keep watch. Easing my way out of the SUV, I do a few exercises to loosen up my stiff body and then slip back in. I lay my head back against the seat and instantly notice the thick blanket of stars. They're beautiful and so bright that even the weak parking lot lights can't block them from view. They're absolutely glorious. I'm not familiar with many of the Southern hemisphere constellations, but I spot the Southern Cross. My hand goes to the antique silver cross I wear.

I wonder where Andre is tonight? Does he ever think of me? Probably not, or I would have heard from the rat sometime over the last year. I can picture him staying at a grand estate in Italy and involved in some complex scam. He's truly the Artful Dodger all grown up. Tons of charm and wit, but without a scruple to his name. My mind wanders, reliving a few of the special times Andre and I had when we were together. I shake myself mentally. I've got to stop thinking about him. Our...whatever it was...is over and done. Better I concentrate on the bad things he did to me. Time to move on.

An approaching vehicle jerks me from my thoughts.

"That's it," I shake Steve awake and start the motor.

The Coober Pedy Mortuary hearse slows at the intersection and turns into town. I let it move a block ahead and then follow. There's not exactly a lot of traffic to conceal our SUV at the moment.

The SUV's headlights illuminate signs with arrows to the Camel Tours, several restaurants, and the Opal Fields Golf Course. That's a joke, right? We follow as the hearse winds slowly through town and out to the far side. It comes to a stop in front of a door in the side of a low hill. A nearby sign reads -- Inter Faith Church. There's a small cemetery plot adjacent.

"That's an odd looking place," Steve says, referring to the church.

"Probably a dugout. People here live in old caves or mines that are refitted for living. It's to beat the intense heat in the summer."

"I read about those. You think we can go inside?"

"We'll be back tomorrow."

"I read about dugouts in the guide book, but I thought they were exaggerating."

A man emerges from the church. We watch as he directs the unloading of the casket and rolls it inside on a dolly.

"Time to leave. There's no good excuse for us asking questions at this time of night. Let's find our hotel. We'll come back first thing in the morning."

***

"Hey, this is cool." Steve admires our hotel lobby.

The hotel is also a dugout, with soft rose and maroon colored sandstone interior walls. In addition, there's a beautiful swirling texture left by the tunneling machines.

I pause to read a poster about the Coober Pedy Prospector's Festival that Penny mentioned on the plane. Looks like fun, but I hope we'll be gone before the weekend.

Steve heads for the reception desk and the cute young receptionist with bright magenta pixie cut. It might sound odd, but on her it looks adorable.

When she catches sight of Steve, a huge smile crosses her face.

"G'day. I'm Dana Ornet. Welcome to Coober Pedy. How may I help you?"

Another one of those many women who find him attractive. It's amazing he doesn't have a swollen head.

"We called earlier. Two in the name of Harrison please."

"That's for you and your mother?"

Whoa. She thinks I'm that old?

Steve says, "No, she's my sister."

Dana shrugs. "The Prospector's Festival packs the town. You were fortunate we had some last minute cancellations." She looks at me for the first time. "Eww. What happened to your eye?"

Drat. I forgot to put my sunglasses on, again.

"It's okay. I was hit by a door."

She tilts her head and continues to stare at me. "If you say so," she says, not buying my explanation at all.

"It's true," Steve says. "It opened suddenly. Bam. Caught her right in the face."

Him she believes.

She says to him, "Be sure to let me know if I can help you. Again, my name is Dana. Here, your rooms are right this way." She spots Steve's boomerang. "Cool, you brought a boomie. Do you know how to use it?"

He shakes his head.

"I can give you lessons if you like."

"Sure. How about tomorrow?"

"Right, then." She wrestles his backpack from his hands before the two of them head down the hallway, leaving me to carry my own bag and follow. I'm only thirty-four. How can a twenty-year-old make me feel so ancient?

CHAPTER ELEVEN

My phone alarm goes off at dawn. I roll out of bed into my clothes. Cargo pants and a tee-shirt with a kangaroo on the back courtesy of the airport gift shop. I meet Steve in the hall. He's also wearing an outfit purchased at the airport. We definitely look like tourists.

"I never slept anywhere this quiet," he says.

"Me neither." The expression "quiet as a grave" crosses my mind. I involuntarily shudder. It doesn't help that I feel vulnerable without my Glock. We are in wild country. Plus people who make off with three million dollars are apt to be resistant about giving it back. This trip was too fast. I had no time to organize the shipping of my gun or arranging to buy one here.

I tell myself that maybe it's for the best. Anything that might make the police notice my name should be avoided.

With my sunglasses firmly in place, we head out through the hotel lobby in search of breakfast. As we near the entrance, a voice calls out from nearby. "Lexi? Lexi, dear. How fun. We're staying in the same place."

It's Penny, my seatmate from the airplane. A surprise, but I guess it is a small town.

She waves and hurries over. "How are you? She frowns when she notices Steve. "Is this your husband?"

Hmm. She has a good memory. I can see she's thinking about my black eye and I only mentioned Steve once.

I introduce Steve. Big mistake. I barely manage to drag him away after Penny delivers a fifteen minute list of things we should see or do while we're here.

We pause outside the entrance. It's early, but the sun is up long enough to warm the air. Today will be a hot one. It's our first, real daylight view of the dry, barren desert town known as Coober Pedy. We pause to look around. I knew what to expect, but it's still a shock.

We can see the town off to one side of our hotel. Rusted out cars seem to be the preferred lawn ornament. The above ground homes and businesses are mostly one story. Grass and trees are non-existent. They're replaced by white, three foot high, capped ventilation pipes standing vertically from every hill above underground homes -- like some strange, tall, skinny mushrooms.

Steve stares, speechless.

A loud rumble makes us turn in the opposite direction.

Outside of town is a landscape that could rival Mars. In fact, I understand it's even been used by film makers in movies about Mars.

As far I can see there are four foot wide mine shafts dug vertically into the ground with adjacent, upside down, cone-shaped piles of excavated dirt. It's as if a giant gopher colony lives here. There are multiple signs warning "beware of unmarked holes." I'd heard there was a huge number of such mine shafts in the area.

Large clouds of red dust billow behind cars approaching town from the outer areas. Hard to realize this place was an ocean a hundred and fifty million years ago.

"Probably someone mining," I say regarding the rumble.

Steve looks around "Do you really think our three million dollars is here?"

"No idea, but with what we know, it's as good as any place."

"Even if we figure out where it went, how can we recover it?"

"Oh, now you have doubts? Let's find it first. Then we'll worry about how to get it back. Come on. We need to eat before heading back to that church."

***

It's still early when we arrive at the Inter Faith Church after grabbing donuts and coffee from a convenience store. I hope lunch offers better choices. I spotted a place that offers Greek Gyros. Gyros are a favorite of mine. They consist of lamb, chicken, and pork strips topped with onions, tomatoes slices and a special Greek tzatziki sauce packed together in a pita type cone. Yummy. My stomach rumbles in agreement.

I park our SUV a block away from the church where we have an unobstructed view. We sit in silence as we wolf down the donuts. With all the hours sitting on planes and food like donuts, I'm going to have to step up my exercise after I get home.

Since there's only the same car parked in front of the church as last night, we figure it belongs to the minister. We agree we'll wait until there's a bit more activity before we go in.

Steve flips through his guide book to kill time.

A fly lands on my nose. Ugh. I swat at it, remembering that the motion used to brush a fly away from your face in this part of Australia is called the "Aussie Salute." I quickly roll up the windows and adjust my sunglasses. My black eye has faded a little, but it's still better if people don't remember me because of it.

Steve continues reading.

Stakeouts are boring. Andre creeps into my mind again. As a con man, he'd be in his element here. Supposedly the place is loaded with gold, oil, and opals, although art seems to be his favorite target.

"Hey, this church is on the places to see list," Steve says, interrupting my thoughts.

"Great find."

"You don't have to be sarcastic."

"No, really. It's good. That means we don't need an excuse to cover a visit. We're tourists. Let's go sightseeing."

I put the SUV in drive and head toward the church, but before I get there, a white passenger van passes me at high speed and cuts me off. I honk in annoyance.

The driver flips me the bird. Nice.

The van jerks to a stop in a cloud of dust at the church. A stocky, older woman gets out and rushes inside.

I park next to the van and notice there's a sign on its door that says Collins Outback Tours.

Collins? That's curious. It's a common name, but I've seen it recently. Yes, it was in Willis' bank box papers and inscribed in a couple of the books at his house. Ted. Ted Collins. The one I think might be a possible relative or friend of Willis'. Good. Maybe the woman is here about Willis.

As Steve and I enter, we can hear voices echoing through the church's dugout interior.

A woman says, "What's the point of waiting? If the body's here, then say a few words and put him in the ground quick."

A man's voice says quietly, "That's unseemly. Eight tomorrow morning is the best I can do."

"I'm trying my darnedest to do my Christian duty here, but my no-good brother can't be six feet under soon enough to please me."

81

Is she Willis' sister? The one who claimed the body? I don't remember her from the plane. The man's voice drops too low for me hear his response.

I peer into the side room to see who's talking. It's the woman who cut me off. She looks to be in her fifties and tough as nails. The baggy work pants, worn mustard yellow work boots, and the dirty, man's button down wool shirt she's wearing make no allowance for gender. Her face is deeply tanned and lined with deep wrinkles from too many years spent under the harsh sun. I would never have figured her for Willis' sister. Maybe she's a Collins by marriage.

The man must be the minister here. He wears a clean white shirt and dark slacks. About forty, he's slim to the point of skinny, but he has an open, engaging expression.

The woman turns, noticing us for the first time. She angrily brushes past us. Then stops and turns on me. "Who are you?"

"Clare...," the minister cautions.

I refuse to back down. "We're sightseeing. Isn't this a public place?"

"Clare," the minister says more forcefully.

She throws him an annoyed look and leaves.

"How can I help you folks?" The minister asks, his smile warm and inviting.

"We didn't mean to interrupt anything."

"No, no. Nothing important."

"Your church was mentioned in our guide book."

"Come in. I'm Martin. The rock carvings on our walls will be what you want to see. This way. Let me show you around. We're one of the older churches in the area. The carvings were done back in the eighties and are what most people come to see. There's another church in town you shouldn't miss. It has even older carvings."

He gives us the tour. It's fascinating, but not why we're here. Luckily, it's short because there are only four public rooms. As we're saying goodbye, I ask, "Would you happen to know a Creiger family?"

He pauses, trying unsuccessfully to hide his surprise. "In Coober Pedy? Can't say as I do. I think I'm familiar with most of the people in town. At least their names. Are they new?"

He's lying. I can tell, but I decide not to call him on it...yet. Instead I say, "I've probably got the name wrong. A friend asked me to say hello if we visited here. Would it be all right to come back tomorrow to take pictures of the rock carvings? They're truly lovely."

"Any time late in the afternoon. Where are you staying?"

"At the Ornet's," says Steve, before I can stop him.

"Nice place. Will you be in town long?"

"A week or two."

At that point I manage to catch Steve's attention to stop him talking.

We thank Martin for the tour and head back to the car.

"That was odd," Steve says.

"Yes, and he didn't want us to come back until after the morning funeral."

"Makes sense in a way. You don't want lookee-loos at a funeral."

"True, but I wonder if there isn't more to it."

***

We exit the church and are immediately attacked by a swarm of huge flies. They crawl on our faces forcing their way into our ears, eyes, and noses. Yuck.

Fighting them off, we race to the SUV. Unfortunately a number of the flies make it inside with us. For five minutes, we battle the aggressive bugs. When it's over, there are squashed flies all over the dash, seats, and windows. Digging out tissues, we mop up the bodies.

"Where did they come from?" asks Steve.

"I guess the sun warmed up enough to make them active. The outback is famous for its fierce flies."

"There's nothing in the guide book about flies."

"Probably deliberate. Or tourists wouldn't come. Uluru Rock, a ways north of here, is notorious for the flies."

I reach for the bag of my purchases from the airport gift shop on the back seat.

"Here." I hand him a khaki hat with a heavy fly net and remove one for myself.

"Neat."

"Looks like we're going to need them."

"How can Martin not know Willis Creiger?" Steve asks. "We know his body is in that church. We didn't lose his casket, did we? I mean, we didn't actually follow it. Could Willis' hearse have gone to another city and a different hearse come here?"

Anything's possible, but I certainly hope not. Still, tomorrow will be a first for me. I never crashed a funeral before.

CHAPTER TWELVE

Morning finds us parked a block away from the church again. Luckily the area isn't residential. Only one car has passed in the last hour. We have a clear view of the workmen in the cemetery arranging chairs around an open grave.

We spent yesterday afternoon blending with all the real tourists here for the Prospectors Festival. We walked around town, ate gyros, bought good hiking boots, jeans, polo shirts, and necessities. Then we checked out the elevated opal drilling rig that tops a huge Coober Pedy sign at the entrance to town. We asked everywhere we went if anyone knew the Creigers. Not one person ever heard the name.

Steve had a boomerang lesson with Dana and returned with a new bruise on his cheek. With my black eye and his cheek, people must think we've been fighting. I make sure my sunglasses stay firmly in place.

I fold the local paper I bought at breakfast.

"There's no notice of a funeral for Willis today," I say.

"That's odd."

True.

After the funeral, I plan to ask people about the names on Willis' papers, Ted Collins, Joan and Emily Lassiter.

***

It's seven-forty-nine when the white Collins' Tour van parks at the church. The woman who may be Willis' sister, Clare, gets out and enters the church. Then a rusted out Toyota Land Cruiser, an ancient Chevy, an older model Prius, and several decrepit pick-up trucks, known as utes in Australia, drive up and park. From our vantage point, we can't see who gets out of all of them, but that's it for attendees. We're surprised when no more vehicles arrive.

"That's it?" Steve asks.

We leave our SUV and slip into the church, staying in the vestibule outside of the door to the main room where we can listen without being seen. Martin has already started the service.

Taking a quick peek inside, I can only see the back of people's heads. I note the maybe sister is still wearing the same clothes as yesterday. Not exactly respectful attire for a funeral. Then there's an attractive, gray-haired man in his sixties. He's also wearing rough work clothes. Maybe funerals are considered casual here.

I look to the next person and do a double take. It's the heavily bearded guy with the inappropriate sunglasses from the plane. Maybe it doesn't mean anything and he was coming from Melbourne for the funeral. He has an angry expression on his face and gazes all around the church, apparently disinterested in the service. He's wearing a dark suit, as is the nice looking blonde man in his late thirties beside him.

Across the aisle from them sits a man with a little girl. He's in his mid to late thirties with dark chestnut colored hair...No, it can't be. The hair color is different, but I'd recognize that profile anywhere.

I jerk back out of sight. How can he be here?

Steve sees the pale, strained look on my face and whispers, "What's wrong?"

I shake my head. I must be hallucinating. It's a good thing I'm leaning against the wall because my knees feel like jelly.

I look again. It can't be. And who is the little girl? Is she his daughter? Is he married? How can that be? I scan the room again, but don't see the man or the little girl. Was it my imagination?

My heart is beating so loudly, I can barely hear what Martin is saying.

"... a person we love passes on, we feel an element of loss. If you've been around someone for years, that person has become an important part of our lives. It's natural to miss them--"

The Collins tour woman snorts loudly. A man snickers.

Martin frowns, then continues. "But today, beyond our natural sorrow, there is a joy that comes from knowing the reality of God's love and his divine forgiveness. As we lay Willis Creiger to rest..."

Steve and I exchange a look. Why did Martin claim not to know Willis?

I venture another glance, but people are starting to rise. I grab Steve and we dart outside, retreating toward the cars. Workmen wheel Willis' coffin out of the church and towards the cemetery. People stream outside and trail behind Martin as he follows the casket.

Everyone exits except the man with the child. Where did they go? Is there a side door? Did I really see them?

Keeping our distance, Steve and I tag along behind the mourners, although that's not a word I'd use to describe this group. You'd think they were on a picnic, laughing and chatting. The workmen stop next to the freshly dug grave.

The flies are back. Several people do the Aussie salute, including me.

I scan the group carefully. There's no mid-thirties man with dark chestnut hair or a little girl. I don't know if I'm relieved or disappointed.

Martin says a few words, "Dust to dust, ashes to ashes..."

Quickly the workmen lower the coffin and begin to

shovel dirt over it. With the service over, people hurry past us and back to their cars. One guy's even cracking jokes. I notice the rusted out Land Cruiser is gone.

Now I'm mad.

Steve is getting good at reading my expressions. "What?"

"These people are supposed to be Willis' friends and family. That had to be the worst and the shortest funeral ever. That's pretty callous treatment. Look at the grave. Not one flower."

Martin notices us and catches the Collins woman's attention. Her head jerks sharply in our direction. She exchanges words with Martin and heads to her truck. Martin approaches us with a wary expression. "Can you come back later? This isn't a good time. We're finishing a private event."

"Sorry, we didn't mean to intrude," Steve says.

"Best you leave."

"I thought you didn't know Willis Creiger." Steve blurts.

Martin gives us an angry look. "I don't know who you are, but you need to stop asking questions." He turns and strides into the church.

"What was that all about?" Steve asks as we head to our car.

I shake my head as I absently swat a fly. "I think a research trip to the local newspaper office is in order."

CHAPTER THIRTEEN

After the weird reaction we got from Martin when we asked about Willis, and since this is a small town, I decide not to directly ask for information about him at the newspaper office.

We approach a tall, frumpily dressed woman with cigarette stained hands, and nicotine breath who stands at the counter. I ask if she has files from the couple years before Willis seemed to magically appear in California.

"Sure," she says. "Anythin' particular you're lookin' for?"

"No, just general local information."

She gives me a suspicious look. "You're not planin' on tryin' to collect the reward are you?"

"Reward?"

"That was the year of the bank robbery. Lots of folks come in here lookin' for clues to Ted Collin's whereabouts."

I'm startled to hear the name Ted again. "We met a Clare Collins yesterday. Are they related?"

"Yeh." The woman catches my reaction and smirks.

"What robbery?" Steve asks.

She's not buying for a second that we don't already know. "You can use the reference computer over on that desk," she says. "Put in the dates you want."

She strolls over to an elderly man at a desk in the rear of the office where the two have a chat. One which includes frequent glances in our direction.

I type in the year and then, since I'm curious now, bank robbery. There's only one robbery comes up, an aborted one where a bank guard was killed, the two thieves got away, but without any money. A gun dropped at the scene was proved to be the weapon that fired the fatal shot. It was registered to Ted Collins. The second man is unknown. A warrant was issued for Ted's arrest.

Steve and I exchange a look. "Definitely a relation to the woman with the tour van," he says.

I have a sad thought. "Remember all the documents Willis had for Ted Collins? Could Willis have been the unidentified man? At the very least, they must have known each other. That would also account for a sudden desire to leave Coober Pedy."

I sense the newspaper woman walk behind us and then move on to the water cooler on the far side of the room.

She was definitely trying to see what we were reading.

Then I recall the books at Willis' house about Stingaree and Ned Kelly. I knew they were bank robbers, one fictional and one real, but forgot they were Australian bank robbers. And like American bank robbers Bonnie Parker and Clyde Barrow, they were folk heroes.

Who knew Willis was an embezzler and Ted is a murderer. Interesting that an embezzler and a murderer are...were friends. It even sounds like the beginning of a bad joke. An embezzler and a murderer walk into a bar...

But there's no mention of Willis Creiger in any of the newspaper articles we're reading. Ted and his unidentified accomplice were never found even though there is a twenty thousand dollar reward posted for information leading to their capture.

Apparently the victim, Vicente Vasco, was well liked. There was a huge public outcry to locate his killers.

The newspaper woman passes behind us again on her way back to her desk.

I wonder if Ted Collins could possibly be the bearded man from the plane and do a search on Ted Collins. No pictures appear, but there are lots of articles about him.

As a young man, he had lots of minor scrapes with the law, but nothing serious. Things like speeding on his motorcycle, stealing camels with his mates and racing them through the center of town, getting drunk and disorderly. Usually in the company of another young man named

Andy Van Brugge. In later articles, Van Brugge disappears and Riley Pettersen replaces him as Ted's apparent best friend. Not good, but seemingly normal hi-jinks for high-spirited teenagers with no other outlets for their energy. There's nothing in the records we read that indicates malice or that one day Ted would become a felon.

Finally there's an article with a picture of Ted Collins attached.

Steve and I stare in shock.

Ted Collins is Willis Creiger.

We sit in silence, trying to process the information. Willis is, was, a murderer with a price on his head.

We jump when the newspaper woman's voice comes from directly behind us. "Thought you folks weren't interested in the robbery?"

"We're not, but it keeps popping up," I say in an effort to cover. "Must have been big news at the time."

"Vicente was a popular bloke with lots of close mates. He had a sweet wife and three darling kiddies. There was even talk about hanging that rat bag Ted Collins and his mate as soon as they were caught."

"Was the other robber ever identified?" I ask.

"Nope. The two of them got clean away. Tough on the Collins family though. The whole town figures they know where he is. Either them or that wife of his. Still have a lot of hostility directed their way."

"Wife?" What else don't we know about Willis?

She gives us a cold look. "Thought you folks weren't here about the robbery?"

"It is interesting, like you said," I manage to utter while still trying to recover from Ted and Willis being the same person. "It must have been a terrible event for everybody involved."

She gives a snort. "This is our early day. We close for lunch in another half hour."

After she moves away, we continue reading the articles about Ted Collins. The articles say he has an older sister named Clare and an older brother named Kenneth, as well as dozens of cousins, aunts, and uncles.

The Collins family shows up as boisterous and brawlers. At least one or two members appear in articles constantly, usually on their way to jail. They're quick with their fists and opinionated about everything. Where were all those relatives for Ted's funeral today? One article says Ted's sister, Clare, started the Collins Outback Tours about ten years ago and her company is well regarded, even though the family isn't.

Before we finish, I type in Joan and Emily Lassiter. The only thing that comes up is a single line announcing the marriage between Joan Lassiter and Ted Collins at the Inter Faith Church. Martin totally lied.

We thank the newspaper woman as we leave. Her eyes narrow as they follow us out the door.

Steve and I take away the unsettling information that

nothing we know about Willis is correct. We fall into silence, each with our own thoughts about the day's discoveries.

As we get in our SUV, Steve asks, "So if Ted Collins and Willis are the same person, why did Ted's family bury him as Willis?"

"Based on what we just heard, my guess is they wanted to bury him in the family plot secretly, so as not to stir up the animosity of the community and questions from the police. It would also explain Martin's efforts to keep the funeral a secret."

"Whoever murdered Willis...Ted, knew he was in the States."

"I wonder if it was his partner from the robbery."

"Possible. Another good question is since Clare Collins was the only adult woman at the funeral, where was Joan Lassiter? Surely his wife should have been there."

***

Steve and I grab a late lunch and decide to tour the town for a couple hours to keep up our pretence as tourists while we consider our next move. I'm thinking we should learn more about Joan, his wife.

We visit the usual must-see places, such as the Umoona Mine and Museum which is actually inside an old mine.

The museum has glass case after glass case of gorgeous opal jewelry in brilliant colors. I'm not a big jewelry person, but many of the pieces are truly works of art by both jewelers and nature. I can barely manage not to drool all over the jewelry cases.

A saleslady tells us that a bright opal is worth more per carat than a diamond. And we laugh out loud when we learn that Coober Pedy, in a dialect of the Aborigine language, means "white man in a hole."

The museum fascinates me. I would enjoy it more except for having the creepiest feeling of someone watching us. With all the other tourists milling in and out, it's hard to spot anyone in particular.

The opals on display inspire us to try our hand at "fossicking." It was one of the items my airplane seatmate, Penny, said was a must do. We ask the saleswoman to direct us to an appropriate spot. She tells us of one right on the edge of town.

Steve reads from his guide book. "Fossicking is digging through the tailings or mullock piles of debris excavated from the opal mines. Miners aren't interested in the lower grade opals, but frequently good opals are overlooked in the removed dirt." Apparently it's a popular pastime for tourists and locals at mines that allow it. We follow directions to the mine and pay our ten dollars to dig. But after a hot, dirty hour and three broken nails worth of digging, I manage to find one tiny opal with a little blue color. Steve fares better. He locates two small pieces of white opal and one microscopic one with a bit of green flash in it.

Hot, tired, and dirty, we finally call it a day. My neck is prickling from the feeling of being watched. They must be good because I can't catch whoever it is. I can't imagine who could be interested in us or even have a reason to follow us? If it were the worst case of being the police from Sydney, they'd arrest me outright, not stalk us. Why would anyone be interested in us anyway?

We head back to the hotel.

CHAPTER FOURTEEN

I unlock my hotel room and step in. Before I can switch on the lights, I'm grabbed from behind and the door's kicked shut.

My response is automatic, taught to me at the police academy years ago. There's a rewarding "offf" from my attacker as my elbow jams into his chest. I quickly drop through the encircling arms twist to face my opponent.

But wait. I recognize that "offf."

"Andre?" I ask.

"Lovely to see you, too, Cherie," he manages to gasp in his Dutch accent.

Only one person calls me that. I flip the lights on. It is him. Here? My throat constricts. "Andre," comes out in a whisper. I wasn't hallucinating at the church. I did see him.

His arms go around me, trapping me tight against him. Every sense in my body absorbs his warmth, his smell, his presence. How good he feels.

No, I'm not doing this again. He broke my heart. I won't let him do it again. I step back, putting space between us.

He rubs his sore chest. "Lexi, you have very sharp elbows."

He looks exactly the same as when I last saw him a year ago except for a different hair cut and the chestnut dye. But it's the same crooked smile, the same twinkle in his eyes. Not a conventionally handsome man, but so attractive.

"It's not important. What are you doing here?" I demand.

"I couldn't get over it when I saw you skulking around at the church," He says with his Dutch accent.

"We were not skulking --"

"I'm glad to see you."

He kisses me. And he's a great kisser. My bones melt as well as what's left of my brain.

I push him away. No way he's going to charm me again. "What are you doing here?" I ask.

He looks at my face. His finger comes up and traces my black eye. His touch is like lightning -- straight to my heart.

"Who did that to you?" He asks angrily.

Bam! Bam! Bam! Is that my heart or is somebody knocking?

Andre moves to the side of the door.

Drat. Must be knocking.

Bam! Bam!

"Hey, Lexi. Open up," Steve shouts through the door. "Dana and I are going to practice with the boomie and then go for tucker. That's Australian for food. Cool, huh? You want to join us or should I bring you takeout back?"

Andre shakes his head in resignation, "I see you're still babysitting what's his name. Shall I let him in?"

"Stop it. You know his name is Steve."

"Who's that? Is anyone in there with you?" Steve yells.

Andre yanks the door open, grabs Steve by the shirt, and jerks him into the room. I slam the door shut and feel a little satisfaction at seeing Steve jump.

Steve's frozen, staring at Andre. "It's you."

"Yes." Andre looks from Steve's bruised cheek to my black eye. "Did you do that to Lexi?"

"No, of course not. Tell him, Lexi."

"Stop it, Andre. I got hit by a door. Our bruises aren't related."

I turn to Steve, "What do you want?"

Still staring at Andre, he says, "You shouldn't be here."

"Neither should Lexi," says Andre, "And yet here you are."

"Is this where you've been for the last year?" Steve asks.

"No, but what business is my whereabouts to you?"

"Why are you here?" I ask.

"I came for my friend Ted's funeral," he says.

"You knew Willis...Ted?" I didn't see that coming.

"Sure, and his wife, Joan."

103

"It figures you two crooks are friends," says Steve.

I'm in total shock. "How is it you know them?"

"Joan grew up near me. We went to school together. Ted was a year ahead. I was gone long before they hooked up, but I did receive a note when they got married."

"You're from here?" I couldn't be more stunned then if he announced he was born on Mars.

He nods. "My parents died when I was fifteen, went to live with my relatives, the Van der Meers, in Holland. Why are you here?"

"Ted stole three million dollars from his employer's account at our bank."

"That's ridiculous." He pauses, realizing I'm serious. "Not Ted. He's the most honest and loyal man I know."

"If he's mister honesty, what about the bank robbery here and the murder of the guard?" Steve asks.

"Yes, explain that," I say. Geez, I sound like Steve's echo.

Andre pauses. "Joan and I can't figure that out. It's totally out of character. He's refused to talk about it with her. Then he left the country within hours after it happened. She was hoping he'd open up after he came home this week."

"How did Ted end up in California?" I ask.

"Maybe I helped him with a little paperwork and a new passport. Why?"

"Andre, did the police tell Joan that someone was in

the room when I found Ted."

"You found Ted?" Andre's expression goes ice cold. He stares at me. "The police contacted his sister, but she never told Joan anything like that. I thought he fell and accidentally hit his..."

I shake my head. "I don't know if I agree."

Andre sits me down on the bed. "What exactly happened?"

I give him a replay of what occurred at Ted's house.

"I have to go," Andre says as I finish. He's the angriest I've ever seen him. And, without looking at me again, he opens the door and leaves. Slamming it behind him.

I stare at the closed door. He's gone? This is not the way I imagined it would be if we ever met again. I'm the one who should slam the door on him. I'm furious. Why does he think he can just walk in and out of my life?

But there's a tiny bit of me that's hurt. That part wants to run after him and beg him to come back. Boy, how stupid am I?

"Good riddance," says Steve.

Steve moves behind me, but I feel like I'm in a bubble, totally disconnected from the rest of the world. He lays his hand on my shoulder, breaking the moment.

"Andre has a real nerve thinking he can stroll back into your life after a year of silence. Why are you being so nice to him? I thought you were going to tell him off the next time you saw him."

I'm surprised at the vehemence in Steve's voice.

"That'll have to wait. Did you hear him? He knows Joan Lassister. He could be the key to finding the money."

"You think he's involved?"

"If he, Ted, and Joan are friends, it wouldn't be a stretch."

"You realize there's no possible future for you with him?" Steve says. "Either he's going to be caught and thrown in prison, or one of his victims is going to catch up with him."

I hold up my hand. "Enough," I say. "I'm not that stupid. We need to string him along until we figure out what's going on."

He sighs heavily and shakes his head. No question he disapproves of my relationship with Andre.

There's a loud knock on the door. I pull it open, expecting Andre.

But it's not.

Dana stands impatiently in the hall.

"Seen Steve?" She asks, then spots him behind me. "Hey, you ready to go?"

He looks to me. "Are you sure you're going to be using him and not the other way around?"

Good question. Am I being truthful about exploiting Andre to find the money? Or am I lying to myself?

CHAPTER FIFTEEN

In the early morning hours, I'm still tossing and turning, unable to sleep. I keep replaying my meeting with Andre over and over in my head. Why did he run out like that? Why is he really here? Is he involved? It seems likely. How handsome he looked... I hear someone in the hall pause in front of my door. Probably Steve and Dana coming back late or another hotel guest. Still, I hold my breath hoping that maybe it's Andre making one of his nocturnal visits. I don't bother to get out of bed and see. I know the lock will be child's play if it's him. He'll let himself in like he did earlier. I smile remembering one of the last times he came to my room late at night in Sumatra.

In the pitch black, he'd removed all of his clothes between the door and the bed. Unfortunately, a friend of mine was sleeping in my bed at the time. Her screams brought me from the room next door and the look on both their faces as I flipped the lights on is one of those memories I'll never forget.

After a moment, whoever it is moves away, walking quietly back toward the reception desk. Disappointed, I roll over and try to sleep.

Half an hour later, I'm finally dozing off when I feel a weight move across my foot. I freeze. The weight moves but doesn't seem to end. It's headed up the right side of my body.

I gather all my courage, throw my blankets to the right and over it, and roll off the bed to the left. I instantly rush for the door and hit the light switch beside it and look back.

Slithering from under my blankets is a huge eight foot snake, angrily flicking its tongue.

I grab my robe and escape into the hall, slamming the door behind me. Snakes give me the heebie-jeebies. I quickly stuff my robe into the crack beneath the door to trap the snake inside.

I guess I don't mind snakes so much unless they're poisonous. Trouble is I can't tell the difference. Poisonous or not, there's no way I'm sharing my bed with one.

Steve's head pops out of his room. He manages to pretend I'm not standing there naked, bless his heart, and asks, "What's up?"

"I had an unexpected visitor. A snake."

"Andre came back?"

Steve's deadly serious. I can't help it, I start to laugh.

CHAPTER SIXTEEN

"We never lock the main doors at night and, no, we don't have any cameras. We've never needed them." Dana's father, Tom, is gaunt and has a gravely voice. He's clearly annoyed. "Yeh, it's bonkers a snake wandered under your door, but this is the outback. Strange things happen."

It's not that strange. It had human help. I give up. I explained three times that I heard someone at my door. I'm exhausted from lack of sleep and I can barely stand up. I shiver in Steve's bathrobe, but not because I'm cold.

We stand in the hall as the snake wrangler Dana called in tries to capture the snake in my room.

After a tense wait, the disheveled, fifteen-year-old, freckled-faced wrangler finally emerges with an excited look on his face. "It's a beaut," he says. "An eight foot Inland Taipan with a big bonus. She looks pregnant."

He proudly holds up the container confining the

annoyed snake. It flicks its tongue angrily.

We all take a quick step backwards.

"Now, now," the wrangler coos to the snake, "I have a nice home for you and the little nippers. You're a bloody bonzer." With a nod to us, he happily disappears toward the entrance.

Steve looks at Dana, "Bloody bonzer?"

"Very good," I say.

"I didn't know you spoke Australian," Steve says.

"It's not a language. It's slang."

Dana says, "You may not know, but Inland Taipans are only the most poisonous snakes in the world."

I glance at Steve. His face is suddenly as ashen as mine feels.

CHAPTER SEVENTEEN

The sun is barely coming up as Steve and I slip into the last open booth. Even though it's early, the restaurant is already packed with tourists wearing costumes for the Prospectors Days events. Everyone's in a festive mood. There're even people in kangaroo costumes. Thank goodness there's no one in a snake outfit.

One thing I'm sure of. Whoever stopped outside my door last night was responsible for the snake. I take a sip of my coffee. But who and why? Only one person would react to my presence with such a vicious response. Someone who knows or guesses why we're really here. That thought makes me smile.

Steve notices and frowns. "What's with you looking all happy? You could have been killed last night."

"Isn't it great."

He looks at me like I'm crazy. "Lexi, that was a close call. If that snake had --You said yourself the chances are slim we'd find the money. Let's go home. It's not worth dying over this."

"Our chances of finding the money just went from zero to ninety. Who do you think wants us dead? Who could possibly know we're here because of the missing money?"

"Andre?"

I shake my head. "Maybe Ted's killer got a better look at me than I did of him at Ted's house. What if he saw me yesterday -- here in Coober Pedy? What would he think?"

Steve brightens, "He'd think you were on his trail."

"Right. We were thrashing around in the dark. Now he's made a big mistake. He's told us he or she is here."

Steve smiles.

"If he made one big mistake, he'll make another." I add.

Steve's smile disappears. "You expect another attack?"

"I'm counting on it."

"Stop. Listen to me. This isn't worth getting yourself killed."

"You're right," I answer. "No sense in both of us being in Coober Pedy. You should go home."

"Let's both go home."

"No way. Now I know he's here, I'm going to find him."

I look up as Andre unexpectedly enters the restaurant. He looks so handsome in his dark aviator sunglasses and bush ranger hat that I can't wipe a smile off my face. I'm not the only one who notices. Other women turn to watch as he slides into our booth. There's a flash of relief on his face as soon as he sees me.

Steve bristles, but an angry look from Andre backs him off.

"I suppose you heard about the snake in my room?" I ask.

He nods. "I came directly from the hotel. Dana told me."

"Did you tell anyone why we're in town?" Steve asks.

"Only Joan's family."

I shoot Steve a look. "We were asking about Willis Creiger at the church yesterday and you told Martin where we were staying."

Steve's expression falls. "I did, didn't I. He could have told anyone."

Andre ignores him and asks, "How is the poor snake? Should we expect a visit from the animal cruelty people?"

"The snake was alive and well, although a tad irritated. A young man took her away and promised her a good life," I say.

"Tell me."

I keep it short, leaving out that I suspect the attack was based on Ted's killer recognizing me.

Andre takes a few minutes to assimilate the story. "Who would want to hurt you?"

Steve looks pointedly at Andre. "I wonder."

"At Ted's funeral, you saw what the reaction to him

113

was," Andre says. " Local people here, even Ted's own family, hate him for killing the bank guard. Anyone who was friends with him has been ostracized since Vicente's death. Even Joan has to use her maiden name in an effort to disassociate herself and Emily. Maybe your questions about Willis Creiger reached the wrong person. Still, I can't imagine why that anger would transfer to you. Did you tell anyone why you're really here?"

Steve says, "Only you."

"I mentioned to Joan there was a question about Ted's death being an accident or not and told her about you. I knew that would be important to her. I never mentioned the money. She doesn't need to know about that."

"Why not." I ask.

"You'll see."

"Maybe she already knows," Steve says. "Maybe she likes snakes."

Andre gives him a withering look, and turns back to me. "And why you and not the boy?"

"My name is Steve, not boy."

"Joan and I think there's something wrong with the robbery story," Andre says.

I'm hearing a lot of "Joan and I." How close are he and Joan?

He continues "We can't imagine him robbing a bank, much less killing anyone. But I do know one reason Ted might have stolen Mac Parker's money."

"Yes?"

"Later, Cherie."

"What's wrong with now?" I ask.

"I think you should meet Joan and Emily first."

"Who's Emily?"

"Ted's daughter."

"There's nothing I'd like better than to meet both of them."

"We can go right now. She's expecting us. Promise me you won't say anything to her about the money."

"Why not? That's why we're here."

"You'll see."

Again with the "you'll see." Could he be any more vague? No way am I agreeing to that.

CHAPTER EIGHTEEN

Steve and I plan to follow Andre to the Lassiter's, but that's not going to happen.

All four of our SUV's tires and the spare are slashed.

"Good thing you had me buy the rental insurance," says Steve.

"That was for the bad roads," I say. "Not for someone who has serious anger issues."

Steve steps aside to call the car rental people on his cell.

"Definitely a bit of overkill. Looks like someone doesn't want you going anywhere," Andre says. "Each tire has multiple slashes where one of them would have done the job. I'll feel better when we figure who's doing this."

"Seems pretty amateurish. First a snake, now the tires."

"Listen to me, Cheri. You could end up dead even if the perpetrator is not a professional."

"I don't know anyone here...except you."

"Do I need to convince you I didn't do this?"

"No, of course not," I say.

Steve turns back in time to hear. "You can convince me," he says.

Andre ignores him and asks, "Think about it. Who knew you were coming here?"

"Steve's father knew we were coming. That's it."

Steve interrupts us. "A mechanic will be here in a couple hours with new tires. They want us to fill out a police report for the insurance company."

"Maybe you should have stayed in the States," says a deep voice behind me. I turn, coming face-to-face with the tall, heavily bearded man from the plane and funeral, or rather, my face-to-his chest. He was so quiet on his feet, I hadn't heard him approach.

"What's with the face fungus, Kenneth? How many years ago did you lose your razor?" Andre asks.

Andre makes me snicker. Kenneth gives me a malevolent look and turns back to Andre.

"Something about beards you don't like, Andre?"

"Not unless you're hiding behind it while you're slashing tires."

"Wish I'd thought of it first," he says. "Heard you were looking up information on the robbery. Bloody reward hunters aren't welcome here."

"They're friends of mine," Andre says, squaring off. "And not after the reward."

"So you say. You're not exactly high on my list either, you bloody wanker." With that he turns away.

"How was your trip to California, Kenneth?" I call after him.

He pauses. "Never been there." And walks on.

"That guy was spooky. Who is he?" asks Steve.

Andre confirms my guess. "That was Kenneth Collins. Ted's older brother."

"He was on our plane from Adelaide." I say.

Andre shrugs.

"What's a bloody wanker? Face fungus?" Steve asks. Andre doesn't bother to answer.

"If I didn't know better," I say, "I think the Collins family doesn't like us."

Penny, my plane seating partner, and two of her friends exit the hotel and cross the parking lot. Since another car blocks our rental from her view, she waves and they continue on their way without noticing the flat tires.

"Come on, Cherie. We can take my car."

Using my cell phone, I walk around our SUV first and snap pictures of the slashed tires.

"Steve, you better stay and file the police report. Andre and I shouldn't be around when they arrive," I say.

"Can't it wait until we get back? I'd like to meet the Lassiters, too."

"The police should see the damage before the tires are changed or moved."

Steve points at Andre, "Are you sure he didn't do this himself to get you alone?"

Possible, but I hope not. I hand him the SUV keys. "If I'm not back in a couple hours..."

He nods and stares at Andre, "Don't worry. I'll find you."

Andre leads me to his older model Land Cruiser -- as in way older.

"Is it me or is the boy becoming more protective?"

"Could be."

"Good. I'll feel better that he's with you."

We get in and exit the parking lot. The motor sounds like it's going to blow up or die any minute.

There are dents here and there and spots where the body is rusted all the way through. I remember seeing it at the church parking lot.

"Is it safe?" I ask.

Andre's lips move, but I can't hear him.

He reaches under the dash and appears to press a button. Suddenly the rough motor noise disappears. Now the motor sounds like a high powered engine running as smooth as silk.

"The motor noise is a recording," he says. "Makes people underestimate my car. Also helps me blend in when I'm in Australia. The body may be rough, but the engine works perfectly. This vehicle is very dear to me. I rebuilt it right before my parents died."

An image of the detective from Sydney pops into my head. "You don't really think D.I. Brode would ever come here?" I ask.

"Not unless he got really lucky. But I have other enemies..."

"Andre, I've had the feeling that someone is watching us, almost since we arrived."

He gives me worried look. "Your instincts are pretty good. But did you ever think it might be because you're a beautiful woman?"

He laughs at the glare I give him. "Don't try to deny it," he says. "You are."

I wonder what Andre even sees in me. I'm not beautiful or even pretty. A portrait painter I dated once called me endearing, fascinating, and exciting, but I can't count that. He was trying to lure me into his bed at the time.

Andre puts the vehicle into higher gear and we leave Coober Pedy behind us. Rough isn't quite the word for Andre's Land Cruiser. The rattling of the body makes conversation hard. The absence of springs makes for a rough ride and the lack of air conditioning makes us sweat as the day heats up. Low profile indeed. At least flies can't keep up with the moving vehicle.

"We did annoy Martin at the church," I say. "He threw us out."

Andre dismisses Martin with a shrug. "Well, somebody

is certainly unhappy about your presence. What have you done since you got here? And don't omit anything."

"We've asked around town about Willis Creiger, but didn't get anywhere. At the newspaper office, we found out that Willis was really Ted Collins and that's why no one knew the name Creiger."

"You just didn't ask the right people and that's a good thing. I knew who Willis Creiger was," says Andre. "And Ted's family knew."

"And the Lassiters?"

"Right. And a few others."

"Why was Martin that pissed off at us at the church? We only asked if he knew Creiger or the Lassiters."

"Anyone connected to Ted has been barraged by reward hunters. I only learned what was going on after I got here yesterday. Ted was trying to save enough to...well, you'll see."

This meeting better be soon or I'm going to grab a rock and beat the answers out of him. I've had it with "You'll see."

CHAPTER NINETEEN

Many more mine shafts are visible with their upside down, cone shaped piles of excavated dirt beside them as we drive. The landscape is pretty wide open, but I notice Andre keeping an eye on the rear view mirror.

On the edge of the road, we pass an abandoned refrigerator. It makes me smile. The owner has placed a sign on it which reads -- 'I used to be cool.'

The dead refrigerator doesn't equate to a catastrophic event, but it makes me remember an incident years ago. I was checking an insurance claim in Kansas for a house torn apart by a tornado. The devastated, but resilient owners had dug up enough humor in the face of their financial ruin to post a sign in their front yard that read -- Gone With The Wind.

I've seen similar bits of humor at other American natural disasters sites and I've come to love the courage of desperate people who dig deep down to see hope and humor in the face of personal catastrophe. I had thought that was an American trait. Now I see it's another thing we share with our Australian friends.

Moments later, we pass the local drive-in theater. The sign at their entrance reads -- Explosives Are Not To Be Brought Into This Theater.

Does that mean that there are other theaters where explosives are allowed? Or that the local miners carry stuff like dynamite around in their cars?

Andre gives me curious looks as I laugh out loud at the idea. I guess since there are a lot of people involved in excavating here, both are possible.

We continue on for another fifteen minutes before Andre turns toward a small escarpment and the road becomes even rougher. I can see several neglected homes against the base of the slope. Wind and time have taken a toll here.

Andre pulls the Land Cruiser in at one house and stops near several parked cars. I give him a sharp look as I recognize the white Collins tour van parked between an old ute and a beat-up Prius. After a short pause to let the trailing dust from our vehicle's arrival blow past, we step out.

Standing in the Lassiter's rocky front yard, I gaze across the vast desert that fills the horizon. There are several large escarpments in the distance with no visible sign of humans except for the few homes clustered here.

The blue sky above fills my mind's eye. The landscape is awesome in an austere, desolate way. Beautiful, but what a lonely place to live.

Andre prods me toward the Lassiter's door. It opens as we approach and a little girl in pretty pink overalls races out yelling, "Uncle Andre, Uncle Andre." She makes a beeline for him. He scoops her up in his arms. It's the child who was at the funeral with him. From what Andre said, she must be Ted's young daughter, Emily Lassiter.

I'm surprised to see the pleasure on his face. I guess I'd never thought of him with children. I realize how little I know about his life. Does he like football or soccer? Have a dog? Where did he go to school? Has he ever been married? Have children of his own? The list of what I don't know overwhelms me. I stagger slightly.

He grabs my arm to steady me and gives me a questioning glance.

"Thanks. I tripped."

Clare and Kenneth Collins exit the house. They spot us and angrily approach.

Clare confronts me, waving her finger in my face. "You have a nerve coming here. I heard all about you being sneaky at the newspaper office and trying to pry out information on Ted. Go bloody back where you come from and leave us in peace." She tries to stare me down, but I've faced worse.

Andre interrupts. "She has nothing to do with that,

Clare. Back off." "Then why is she here? Nobody comes this far for nothing. She's been stirring up things, asking questions all over town." She turns back to me, "Don't you even think about collecting that reward. Bad things might happen to you."

"I apologize if I caused any problems," I say. "I didn't understand the situation. Ted left a bit of unfinished business at work that needs answers and --"

"-- and what? You thought he'd rise up out of his coffin and satisfy you?" She snarls "Liar" at me and pushes past, heading for her van.

Kenneth follows saying, "Go home. There's nothing for you here."

As they drive off, a woman appears in the front door. She can't be Joan. She's fifty and wearing a frilly old fashioned apron over her modest skirt and top. Even in this heat her blouse is buttoned up to her throat. Her expression is stern, but a smile breaks out as she spots Andre. The smile falters a bit when she sees me, but it returns after Andre puts his arm around her and gives her a hug.

"Morning, Gale. I brought a friend I thought Joan might like to talk to. This is Lexi. She's from the States. This is Joan's mother, Gale Lassiter. Gale, Lexi has some news about Ted's death."

I nod in acknowledgement, but Andre misses that Gale gives me a look that could shrivel granite. She opens the door wide and stands back to let us enter. Andre leads the way, still carrying Emily. I uncomfortably follow.

A soft feminine voice calls out, "Andre is that you? We're in the back room."

I follow Andre and Emily toward the voice and come to a small, comfortable family room.

I pause in the door way, startled. Whatever I expected, this wasn't it. And I do -- finally -- see.

A woman I recognize from the old photo I found in the book of her with Ted, sits on a chaise lounge with her legs covered by a blanket. She wears a scarf over her head in an attempt to hide her severe hair loss. She was beautiful in the photo, but now her face shows deep lines of pain and dark bruising around her eyes. Her skin is pale white and appears that it's almost translucent. Her reddened eyes show she's been weeping, but they light up at the sight of Andre.

Is this Joan? Of all the thoughts I had about her, the idea she was seriously ill never occurred to me.

Seated next to her, holding her hand, is the nice looking blonde man who sat beside Kenneth at Ted's funeral. Joan and the blonde man are in stark contrast. She's frail and weak while he's rugged, deeply tanned, and looks like a guy who spends most of his time outdoors.

Near them is another woman who can only be Joan's sister. She's beautiful and vital. Exactly what Joan had looked like in the picture before she became sick. Her abundant dark hair shines with health and her skin is clear and lightly tanned. Her green eyes widen with pleasure on seeing Andre. She hurries to throw her arms around him in a warm hug.

"I'm glad you're back."

He sets the woman hugging him back a step and makes introductions. "Lexi," he indicates the woman who hugged him, "This is Jean, Joan's sister, Joan, Ted's wife, and Riley Pettersen, a good friend of Ted's."

I smile and shake hands all around. Joan's grip feels fragile. Riley, the nice looking blonde guy, shakes hands with the same vigor as his appearance. Jean's smile is barely welcoming and her grip is surprisingly strong. It makes me notice how good her muscle tone is. I wonder if she's an athlete. Or maybe it's the contrast between her grip and Joan's weak one.

Andre kisses Joan's cheek gently and murmurs a greeting. Emily clings tightly to him the entire time.

Andre senses uneasiness in the room. "What's wrong?" he asks.

"Ted's sister and brother just left," Riley says.

"We saw them," Andre says.

"They were asking if Ted left any money for Joan and Emily. Claimed they had a right to it because of the cost of his funeral and all the grief he caused them," Riley says.

I would not like to be on the receiving end of the furious look on Andre's face. "They dared to say that?" He asks.

Jean nods and strokes his arm, "They were very nasty. Too bad you weren't here to deal with them. They wouldn't have dared behave the way they did."

Riley says, "They kept harassing her about life insurance or any other valuables he might have sent for her and Emily. I finally told them to get out."

Interesting questions, I think. Did Clare and Kenneth know about the stolen money?

Tears flow from Joan's eyes. "I didn't tell them that Ted somehow managed to pay off all my doctors bills and sent money in advance for my next operation, before... before --" She stops and more tears appear.

I freeze. Doctor's bills? That's what the stolen money was for? Ted must have been desperate to help his sick wife. I bet he found some round about way to bounce the money around the world and then directly to her hospital for her past and future bills.

"If I hadn't been here, I think they would have tried to seize anything in the place they could carry away," says Riley.

"Over my dead body," Gale says.

"I'm surprised they didn't try to claim the reward on their own brother," Jean adds.

"Riley said the funeral was small and...," Joan says. "And they buried him with the name he used in America. Why would they do that? It's not right."

"Probably to be sure people don't start up about the robbery again," Andre says.

"I wanted to be there." She accepts a box of tissues from Gale.

"Try to relax. Remember what the doctor said," Gale says.

"Did you know Ted was coming home this week?" Joan asks Andre.

He shakes his head. "I came because you called about the funeral."

"He was coming before the next operation. I was finally going to see him again."

Andre and Emily put their arms around her as she tries to stop crying.

"The man was a murderer. He's not worth any more tears," Gale mutters.

I stand awkwardly, feeling out of place and bad for Joan. What a terrible situation she's in.

Jean watches me oddly. When I catch her noticing, she turns away to look out the window.

Riley leaves and returns with a glass of water for Joan. "Say, have you seen any kangaroos yet?"

The Lassiters and Andre roll their eyes.

I shake my head.

Jean says, "Not now, Riley."

"What do you call an angry kangaroo?"

I shake my head again.

"Hopping mad."

Andre actually groans. I don't blame him. How old is Riley? Or at least his sense of humor? Two?

"Hey," Riley says. "That was a good one. Want to hear another?"

"One was too many," says Jean.

Joan looks to me and makes an effort to pull herself together. "Forgive my bad manners, please. Have a seat. Andre says you saw someone at Ted's house the day he died. Please tell me. The American police called Clare because she was listed in his address book. She dealt with everything. I only know what she told me."

They all look at me.

"I was looking forward to seeing him," Joan continues. "But I was afraid he'd be arrested if he came back."

Andre hugs her. I'm proud to see him giving her a lot of support. Maybe a little jealous too. Everyone here knows him better than I do.

Joan asks Andre, "Don't you have the same problem, Andre? Didn't you tell me you're persona non grata here and there's a detective from Sydney who'd like nothing better than to arrest you?"

"Is that true?" Jean asks Andre.

Andre nods. "It's risky for Lexi and me both to be here. Let's not talk about that now. You know going to jail is a big fear of mine."

"You and Ted used to be such nice boys before you

grew up," Gale says disapprovingly. "Thank goodness none of your bad ways rubbed off on Riley."

"Too right," Riley says. "I reckon I'm perfect." His quip makes us all smile.

"I mean it, young man. Better for Joan to have married you."

"Mother, stop it. You're embarrassing Riley," Joan says.

Riley doesn't appear bothered.

"I'm afraid I didn't really know Ted," I say. "We did find a few papers. There is a life insurance policy made out to you and Emily. Unfortunately they're back in my office in the States."

You'd think I had turned blue with fireworks spouting out my ears the way they all stare at me. I catch a split second silent exchange between Riley and Jean.

"Bloody right he should have had insurance," says Gale. "Do you remember the amount?"

I shake my head no. I remember exactly, but it's no one's business except Joan's. "Send them all to me when you're back in the States. I'm helping Joan deal with her paper work," Riley says.

"No. You do too much already," Joan says as she lays her hand on his arm. "I can do this. It'll help keep my mind off things."

"You said papers plural...?" prompts Gale.

"Yes, there were several."

"Just as long as there's insurance," says Gale. "He owes

her that."

"Now, Mother."

"Well, robbing a bank and killing a guard was a bloody bonkers thing to do," Gale says.

The room falls silent for a moment.

The conversation starts up again awkwardly. I answer questions the best I can about Ted's house. Everyone seems surprised by my story of someone hiding in the closet.

Joan cries hard at that point. All conversation comes to a halt. Her sobs fill the room.

I hate to agree with Andre, but I'm not going to be the one to tell her that Ted stole money for her medical bills. It's too cruel. I doubt any hospital would return the money anyway. That means the bank would have to sue them for it. The headlines would be worse than the ones Mac can come up with. Something like "Bank tries to reclaim money used to save terminally ill patient."

Joan struggles to control her weeping. Tearfully, she asks me to continue.

Since I don't have much to add, I tell her about Frosty.

"He has...had a dog?" Joan says. "Emily would love to have him, but the Australian pet importation involves a long quarantine even if they agree to let him come.

"His name is Frosty. He's really sweet," I say. "Don't worry, I'll see he gets a good home."

"You don't need a puppy," says Andre. "You already

have Steve."

He laughs when I shoot him an annoyed look.

Gale leaves the room and Andre, Joan, Jean, and Riley reminisce about Ted and their past growing up together. Apparently, Andre and Ted were inseparable until Andre's parents passed. Riley and Ted became friends after Andre left.

Listening to them talk about their youthful hi-jinks makes me think they were lucky they all avoided jail as kids and survived the crazy scrapes they got themselves into. The idea of trips to Darwin to wrestle crocodiles for fun makes me shudder.

Eventually we say our goodbyes and leave to the sound of Joan crying again. It breaks my heart to hear her. Jean makes a point of kissing Andre in front of me, and then deliberately gives me an odd smile.

Are they an 'item?' I tell myself I don't care.

Outside, Riley hustles to catch up with us before we reach the car.

"Look, Lexi, you'll be sure to fax those papers as soon as you can, right?"

"Of course, no problem."

He turns to Andre and says anxiously, "After Joan has some time to grieve, I plan on asking her to marry me. Ted would have wanted me to watch over her and Emily. I don't earn much, but we can make it. I know she listens to you. Can I count on your support?"

Andre starts to speak and stops. Then he says, "If she agrees, then I'm okay with it."

Riley's body sags with relief. "Thanks," he says. "Say, did you hear the one about --."

"Sorry Riley, we have to go. Another time." Andre hustles me into his Land Cruiser.

CHAPTER TWENTY

We drive back toward Coober Pedy in silence. Both of us are lost in our own thoughts. Mine are about the three million. I confirm with myself that there's absolutely no way I'm going to tell Joan that Ted embezzled the money to pay for her hospital bills. I don't think she has a clue. She has no means to pay it back. It would just cause her more grief and accomplish nothing.

Ted was willing to go to jail to help her. I ask myself, how far I would go to save someone I loved?

Ted killed a bank guard, and was killed himself. Two horrific events, but those are police matters. Even if I found out who -- and as much as I'd love to catch Ted's killer, especially since we know he's here, it's not my business. My job is the money Ted stole from Mac. Now that I know the money isn't recoverable, Steve and I need to go home.

If I report that I can't find the money, Mac would lose

his money. But after all, he's the one who hired Willis and signed him into his accounts. The bank did nothing wrong. Morgan will have to swallow his fear of public censure if Mac does what he threatens. As for me? If Morgan gets his way, I'll be fired, and that means I'll probably never work as a fraud investigator ever again.

It comes down to a choice between Joan and Emily or Mac's bank account and my job. I'd have to be Solomon to solve this problem. But Emily needs her mother. They're the critical victims here. For Mac and the bank, it's only money. As for me, I guess I'll manage to survive somehow. I'll probably lose my new house. Then it occurs to me. Maybe it's not even up to me.

Andre interrupts my thoughts. "What are you going to do?"

"I don't know. I'll have to talk with Steve."

He guesses my thoughts. "No reason to tell him. Pretend you don't know where the money went."

"I won't lie to him."

"It will kill Joan if she finds out Ted stole the money. She'll try to cancel the operation." He continues, "I'd give you the money, but my funds are a little low at the moment. I had to sell a nice watercolor on the cheap to pay for my last minute ticket here. If you can wait a couple months, I can line the money up."

"There's no time," I say. Not with Mac breathing down the bank's neck.

***

It's mid afternoon when we get back. Andre parks in front of the hotel.

"Lexi, there's a special place I'd like to show you tonight."

"I need to talk to Steve. And we need to leave Australia. You should, too."

"I thought I'd stay around for Joan for a couple more days. Make sure she's okay. I was hoping you'd stay. Give us a little time to talk."

"Do you think she'd mind a few more questions?"

He gives me a questioning look. "We can go back tomorrow."

"How about tonight?"

"I had special plans for us tonight," he says. "Come on. A few more days won't hurt."

I'm curious to know what he cares about enough to want to show me. Yet that's not why I'm here. Besides, I tell myself, I'm only using him for his connections to the Lassiters. Right?

"I don't have time for that. I'm here to work. Tonight I need to clear up a couple questions with Joan," I say. "Steve and I need to leave."

I pretend to ignore Andre's disappointment.

***

I spot Steve and Dana talking by the reception desk. Steve's face lights up as he sees me enter the lobby. Dana turns her attention to another guest.

"What happened?" Steve says. "Did you find the money?"

"Let's go back to our rooms," I say.

Once there, I fill him in. Only I don't tell him that I think the money's unrecoverable. He's a good listener and doesn't interrupt until I get to the end.

"Of all the things I expected...," he says. He's silent for a few minutes. "I'm going to have to think about this a bit more. Talk about a catch twenty-two. Poor Joan. This leaves the bank in a bad position."

Me too, I think, but I say, "Andre is taking us back to Joan's tonight. Come with us. I have more questions I want to ask. See what you think."

CHAPTER TWENTY-ONE

With a couple hours to kill before returning to the Lassiters, Steve opts to head out with Dana for more boomie practice.

Andre and I go into town. We stroll up Hutchinson Street. The town seems even busier today for the upcoming event. The flies are out with a vengeance in the hot afternoon temperature. I quickly retrieve my netted hat from my purse and put it on.

We pause to watch a procession of camels carrying tourists that moves single file up the street. An Aborigine, who's my age, sits atop the first camel and waves to Andre. "Hey, mate. Long time. Come by the digs when you can. Ma will want to see you."

Andre waves back. "That's Derain," he says as the camels stride past. "He loves those animals."

"Lexi, Lexi!" A voice calls from above. "Look at me. Can you believe it? I'm riding a camel."

It's Penny, waving her fly hat, and swaying on top of a huge camel.

"You look great," I yell back.

"This is fun. You should try it."

Before I can respond, she's past me, blocked from my view by the camels and their riders following behind her.

"You ever ride one?" Andre asks.

"In Egypt, but horses are more my thing."

"Derain and I used to have great times riding his camels. Back then, Derain worked for the old guy who owned them. When the man passed, he left his entire operation to Derain."

That reminds me of the newspaper articles about Ted and his friends racing the camels through town.

Suddenly I have that creepy feeling of being watched again. I spin to the left and catch Clare standing near her white van. She's staring at me with a venomous expression.

I've had enough of this. I head straight towards her. Before I reach her, she jumps in her van and takes off.

"Forget her," says Andre. "She can't do anything."

I'm not so sure. The snake in my room was hardly a childish prank and a woman could have done it. Same with the attacks on the tires.

Andre and I continue our walk. We pass a hardware store and several small opal shops. Suddenly he drags me into one.

The inside of the opal store is like stepping into another

world. The tiny store is done up with rich jewel colors and silk fabrics, so different from the sandy beige and reddish browns of the desert outside.

The opals on display glitter brightly under mini spotlights. We could be in a shop anywhere in the world -- Paris, New York, Milan.

Andre stops in front of the counter.

"Hey, mate, didn't know you were in town. "Bin a while," says the salesman. The two men hug.

"Afternoon, Neddy," Andre says. "I'd like to see your best opal rings. My credit's still good, right?"

"Always. For the lady? What's your preference? Lightning Ridge or Coober Pedy?"

I recognize Lightning Ridge as the other major mining center for opals that's located northwest of Sydney.

Andre introduces me and asks, "Which do you like?"

"You don't --"

"-- I want to."

"No, they're too expensive."

"Please say yes. It's important to me."

I agree reluctantly, "Coober Pedy then, to remember this trip."

Neddy lifts a tray of rings onto the counter. The gorgeous stones seem to radiate flashes of color under the multiple lights. It's easy to see why they're often worth more per carat than diamonds.

"You know the world's most valuable opal, the

Olympic Australis was found in Coober Pedy," he says.

We spend the next forty-five minutes pleasantly sorting through Neddy's beautiful selection. He knows his opals and tells us the fascinating stories of where and by whom each stone was discovered as he presents them.

Finally, I point to one that's black with flashes of red, yellow, and blue. It's set in an elegant white gold ring that shows the fire in the stone to perfection.

"You've got bloody good taste," Neddy says. "That's one of the nicest stones I've ever had. And it's one of the rare black opals found hereabouts. Coober Pedy black opals are considered extremely valuable. Most black opals come from Lightning Ridge."

"It's breathtaking," I say, looking at Andre.

"Not nearly as lovely as you are," he says as he tries to slide it on the ring finger of my left hand. I switch hands so the ring goes on my right hand.

Again his disappointment is palpable.

My fingers tingle as he closes his hand over mine. "With all my love," he says.

"Andre...," I say.

"Interesting choice," Neddy interrupts. "I set the stone, but that opal was found by someone you know, Riley Pettersen."

"Riley?" Andre asks.

"He found it fossicking. Won't say where of course."

"Steve and I tried fossicking the other day," I say, "We

didn't see any stones like that."

"An opal of this size and quality that's a black opal is a pretty rare find here. Riley was always a lucky bloke."

Andre seems surprised. "Funny he never mentioned discovering such a great stone."

"I probably shouldn't have mentioned it, but since you're mates and all. You know how people are when they make a good find. They're really secretive if they hope to find more in the same place."

"That makes it even more special that it was found by someone we know," I say. "Thank you, Andre."

CHAPTER TWENTY-TWO

Andre and I join Steve and Dana in front of the hotel.

"Did you see the camels today?" Steve asks. "I'd really like to ride one."

They spot the opal ring on my third finger. Steve gives me a questioning look. I shake my head. He tries to hide his relief.

"Bonzer, that's a smashing beaut," says Dana. "Bet it cost a bloody fortune."

Steve examines it silently for a minute. "I should buy an opal for my mother. Can you take me where you got this, Lexi?"

"I know where you can get some great deals, too," Dana interrupts.

"Sure. We can go to several places. I ought to pick up something for my mother and sister since we're here. Are we booked home yet?" I ask.

"No. I was going to ask you," says Steve. "I was hoping

to ride a camel before we leave."

"You should! It's fun." says Dana.

"I have some questions for Joan tonight. We can spend tomorrow shopping for presents. Then it's time to go home." I say.

***

Andre drives us to the Lassiter's.

"What does Joan have? Cancer?" I ask Andre.

"Breast cancer. And they recently found another large spot that needs to be removed."

"The prognosis?"

"Fair to good depending on how quickly the doctors can operate. Gale said without insurance they were so mired in bills that there wasn't enough money to proceed until Ted suddenly sent the money to pay the old hospital bills and all the upcoming costs."

"Then let's hope for a successful outcome."

Later, Andre, Steve, and I sit down for tucker with Joan, Emily, Riley, Jean, and Gale. At least the meal isn't shrimp on the barbie or Steve's head would explode with glee. Instead, he's very quiet tonight. Not his usual out-going self.

Jean grabs the chair closest to Andre and gives me another of her smirks. She turns her back to me while she chats with Andre. Does she think she's making me jealous?

Joan notices my ring. "How lovely."

"We bought it today from Neddy," Andre says.

Joan asks, "Does this mean...?"

"Yes." "No." "No." Andre, Steve, and I answer simultaneously.

That gets chuckles all around, except from Andre. He gives me a hurt look that makes me feel terrible. Suddenly the evening has lost any pleasure for me. I should never have accepted the ring. It was way too expensive a gift, especially when he said earlier money was tight for him at the moment.

"Neddy said you found the stone, Riley," I say.

Riley looks at the ring with surprise. "Yeh, it looks like one I found. He did a nice job setting it. You know this one? Why did the kangaroo hesitate?"

Groans fill the room.

"He didn't want to jump to conclusions."

More groans.

Unless the man is a complete simpleton, how could he forget finding what Neddy called an unusual and valuable stone? Odd, I think.

Jean looks from the ring to Riley and frowns.

"Do you do a lot of fossicking?" I ask him.

"Yeh, the miners miss a lot of bits and pieces."

The conversation gets more general, but the hurt glances I receive from Andre continue to make me feel bad.

Later, I manage to steer the conversation back to Ted and the robbery. I ask Joan, "What exactly do you remember from that day?"

Gale loses the smile on her face. Excusing herself, she

retreats to the kitchen.

"Everything. How could I not," Joan says.

Riley pats her arm. "Are you sure you want to talk about that?"

She nods. "Right before it happened, Ted came out of the bedroom all upset.

He asked me if I'd seen the gun he kept in his closet. I said no. Then he tore out of the house. Half an hour later, I heard about the robbery on the radio. After that, Ted rushed in, threw some stuff in his backpack, and said he'd contact me later. Then he was gone. A month later, he called me from America."

"Was the gun he was looking for the same gun that killed the guard?"

"Yes. The police said it was Ted's. He only had the one."

"And the police never found his accomplice?"

She drops her head in her hands.

"Let's lay off the questions," Riley says. "Joan doesn't need the past dug up again."

"Only a couple more. Riley, did you or Gale see him that day?"

"Nah. I was away up in Brisbane on an errand and stayed over with Jean. Gale was in Sydney visiting friends."

"Who else was Ted close to?" Blank looks all around.

"Was he close to anyone in his family? Clare or Kenny? A cousin?"

"He and Clare were pretty tight, even though he was a lot younger," Jean says. "She's really bitter now. Thinks he disgraced the family as well as her personally. As far as Kenny goes, there was always some sort of brotherly rivalry there. What do you think, Riley?"

"He was the youngest in their family. They were busy doing their own thing and didn't pay him much attention. Maybe he felt neglected."

Gale returns with more beer and lamingtons, a kind of sponge cake dessert with chocolate and coconut.

"How long will you be staying?" Joan asks.

"Not much longer," Steve says.

The conversation changes away from the robbery, becoming subdued for the rest of the evening.

Later on the way home, Andre asks, "What's with all the questions tonight?"

"I'm a bit surprised hearing how close all of you were, yet none of you knew about the robbery beforehand. And no one knew who Ted was close enough to, to be his partner on a robbery. The whole thing doesn't feel right to me. It even seems like it was timed so he and Joan were the only ones of the group in town."

"When you look at it that way, it is weird." He shrugs. "But probably a coincidence. He was pretty impetuous. He was older and kind of the leader. Always the first to suggest doing something."

"Think about it this way. He was murdered in

California on the night before he was returning to Coober Pedy. I thought it was for the stolen money, but if the money already went by wire to the hospital as a prepayment for Joan a day before he died, why was he killed? Did his robbery partner escape to the States with him and not want him to go back?"

"I obtained forged papers for Ted to get into the States. Not for anyone else," Andre says.

"Then here's what I want to know. What if it was someone who's still here and didn't want him to come back?"

Andre and Steve stare at me.

"Interesting...," Andre considers the idea.

"Kenny was on the plane with us," Steve says.

"The idea that Ted had a friend none of you knew is odd," I say. "Did he have a job at the time of the robbery? Somewhere he might have a friend you didn't know?"

"He was working at the mining office of Ainsworth Opals as an accountant," Andre says.

"That's the one place you all weren't normally with him?"

Andre nods.

"Could his bank robbing partner have been from there?"

"It's a big outfit even though most of the people are locals."

"Not all?"

"No, they have another mine at Lightning Ridge and move people around. Sometimes they flew Ted to the office up there."

"It's strange," I say. "A robbery isn't something you embark on with just anybody."

CHAPTER TWENTY-THREE

Last night almost felt like a wake to me. I guess in a way it was. Dawn comes too soon. Steve and I plan to head for home late today. I'd hoped to spending the time remaining working things out with Andre. Instead, he decided to fly last night to the Ainsworth Mine offices in Lightning Ridge. He hopes to find someone who remembers Ted and who might have been close to him and then fly back before we go. I wanted to go with him, but he convinced me it will be easier if he's alone.

Andre and I have a late lunch planned after he comes back and will spend the rest of the day together before Steve and I leave.

Steve and I head for brekkie at our usual restaurant. It's even more crowded than yesterday. We have to wait a few minutes for a booth.

Steve lowers his voice when we're finally seated. "Can

we talk? About the money?"

"Of course."

"Do we have to tell Joan that Ted stole the money for her doctor's bills and we're here to take the money back?"

"It's up to you."

"It doesn't feel right. I don't think we should do it."

"Are you sure?"

"Yes."

Steve never ceases to surprise me. I expected an argument. Instead, his sense of humanity and good heart form his reaction. Those are two things that I really like about him.

"You're absolutely sure you're okay with this?" I ask.

He nods. "It's Mac's problem. Not Dad's, not the bank's. It's not Joan's fault either."

"Well, that's only right then since there's nothing here to discover. After all, it was a silly idea to follow Ted's body anyway."

"Ted who?" Steve winks at me, "Do you know anyone named Ted?"

I laugh. "Never even heard of anyone by that name."

Andre should warn Riley though. He'll need to figure out how to protect Joan if anything happens later.

While I have sympathy for Joan, there's no excuse for Ted murdering the bank guard. I can't forgive that.

Dana joins us in the booth. "You should see Steve with the boomie. He's really getting the knack of it," she says.

Steve beams, "You're a great teacher, Dana." The two of them smile at each other in mutual admiration.

"That's great," I say, pretending interest, but my mind is on my upcoming separation from Andre. I know now that I love him, but is it enough? He's wanted by law enforcement all over the world. Several years ago, he arranged for us to be married in a fake ceremony, then stole a painting and left me alone to face the police. Who does that to anyone they care about? Now I learn Andre's friend, Ted, turns out to be a murderer.

Andre did try to protect me when I was on a case in Sumatra a couple years ago. Only we ended up saving each other. My practical side doesn't see how a long term relationship with him can survive from such rocky beginnings. And yet --

"Lexi?" Steve's voice breaks into my thoughts. "Ready to go look at opals?"

***

We head to Neddy's first. It's his wife who helps us, as he's not working this morning.

Steve selects a lovely piece for his mother comprised of a bright blue opal set in a gold filigree broach. I don't find anything in my budget for my mom or sister. We finish up and follow Dana to another opal store she knows that's a bit out of town.

Dana introduces us to her father's friend, Chip, who works part-time as a salesman there. He's in his mid-fifties.

His deep sunburn makes him look older, but he has a wonderful smile and nice brown eyes. I can tell he's enjoying showing us what's available.

After a bit, I decide on earrings with tiny green opals on a pair of silver crocodiles for my sister, and an expensive opal pendant that's at the limit of my budget. It's set in a contemporary pendant for my mother. I especially picked it because the stone, though much smaller, reminds me of the one in my new ring from Andre.

Chip notices my ring as I hand him my choices to wrap. "Wow. That's pretty smashing."

"Thanks," I say. "I picked this one for my mother because its opal looks similar."

"Possible, I guess. They do have the same colors. This pendant was made from a local find."

"Really? A friend from here found the one in my ring, too."

Chip folds my purchases in tissue. "Who was that?"

"Riley Pettersen."

"You have good taste. My boss bought the stone in this pendant from Riley a couple weeks ago."

"He found it fossicking?"

Chip nods, "He's had the gift lately. He knows the area pretty well, and his luck's been over the moon."

"I thought finding a really good stone was a rare event if you noodle through the...oh what is the mine tailings pile called?"

"The discarded mullock?"

"Right. Isn't it unusual to find even one good opal?"

"A few people who work really hard at it like Riley manage to do okay, but for most, they make money by finding a large quantity of smaller, less valuable stones. A truly top opal like the one in your ring is a pretty spectacular find."

A thought fleetingly tickles my mind, but I can't quite grasp it.

"Riley still dating Jean?" Chip asks.

"You mean Joan," says Steve.

"My bad," says Chip. "Gets confusing since they both have such similar names."

I pay for my purchases. Next we head to a local spot for coffee. It's too warm for hot drink. I'm in luck to find they serve my favorite iced mocha coffee.

"You play golf?" Dana asks Steve.

"My father insisted I learn, but it's not really my thing."

"Have you seen our golf course?" she asks.

"Golf course? It must have lots of sand traps."

I can tell immediately that Dana's heard that one before.

She frowns at Steve. "We could do a round tonight."

"You're serious? There's a golf course?" Steve says.

"We're leaving tonight," I remind him.

"Bummer," Dana says. "You can't miss the golf here. We use balls that glow in the dark," she says. "It's the only course in the world with reciprocal playing privileges with St. Andrews Golf Course in Scotland."

"I haven't seen any place with grass since we got here. How does that work?" he asks.

Good question, I think. I vaguely remember seeing a sign that said golf course.

"You get a piece of artificial turf to tee off on. We go at night because it's cooler. And there's a big bonus. If you find any opals while you're on the course, you're allowed to keep them."

"Has anybody?"

"Lots. One find was worth over three thousand five hundred dollars."

Nice perk, I think. A nice opal beats a hole in one.

"Come on, Lexi," he says. We could move the tickets. Leave tomorrow instead."

I shake my head. "No, it's time we left."

Disappointed, Steve and Dana continue about the unusual local golf course, but my mind wanders back to my conversation with Chip. What was my subconscious trying to tell me?

"Have you ever been down in an opal mine?" Steve asks Dana.

"Oh, sure," she says. "Everyone who lives locally has at one time or another. You want to see one? It's generally a three or four foot wide vertical shaft. You get lowered down in a seat like a bosun's chair or a ladder."

My missing memory hits me. "Steve, the papers we found in the envelope at Willis' house. One was life insurance, and there were tickets and his passport. Wasn't there a couple pages marked deed, license and lease included?"

"Yes. In Ted's name. No, that's wrong. In Joan's and Emily's names."

I grab my cell phone and call back to California. Patricia, the Vice President at our bank, answers. After greetings, I ask her to check the document we found in Willis' house.

"What's going on?" she asks. "I see you and Steve are in Australia. There's no notes from Morgan on why."

"It's personal assignment for him. How's he doing?"

"Fine. It turned out to be stress. They're keeping him for a few more days of observation. Basically he's fine. He'd like an update from Steve."

"I'll tell him. There're a few documents in my left hand desk drawer. Could you please have your assistant photograph them and send them to my phone?"

"No problem. I can do it. I'll call you right back." She hangs up.

I repeat Patricia's information about his father's health to Steve.

He's relieved. "Have her tell him I'll call him later. What's with the papers?"

I wave off his questions. But I can't hide my anxiety,

drumming my fingers impatiently.

Twenty minutes later, my phone rings. It's Patricia calling back. She's sent the photos to my phone. I give her a quick thank you, disconnecting before she can ask any more questions. I quickly pull up the documents on my phone.

"Dana," I ask. "Can you explain please what these documents are?"

She studies them for a minute. "This one is the deed for a piece of property, and the other is a prospecting permit, a license really, and a lease for mineral rights. You have to have one of these special mineral rights permissions if you are going to do any prospecting."

I make another call. This time it's to Joan.

I identify myself and ask, "The property you own out in the desert? Would you mind if I run out and looked at it?"

"You're mistaken. I don't own any property."

"I'm looking at a deed right now in your and Emily's names. Are you sure? Maybe Ted bought it as a surprise?"

"He always talked about buying property, but he never did. Not that I know of. Where did you find this deed?"

"Mixed in the papers at his house."

"Can you bring it by?"

"It's back in the States. Would you mind if I drive past the property?"

There's a pause. Her voice is weaker. "I guess not. Please come by and let me know what you find later. Jean and Riley are here. I'll ask them if they know anything about it."

"Of course."

Good thing she said yes, because I would have gone to look at it even if she hadn't. I only wish Riley wasn't there right now to hear about it.

"Where would we go to find out the location of this property?" I ask Dana.

"It's only a roo hop."

Steve asks, "What?"

"Kangaroo hop. A short distance. That office is right down the street."

"Let's go," I say. We pause only long enough to pay for our drinks and head out, remembering to put on our fly hats as we go.

"What are you thinking?" Steve asks.

"Later. I have a crazy hunch."

We reach the land office and enter.

I ask the clerk for directions to the deeded property. For a fee, she looks it up in her computer, then prints out a map and circles the spot.

While Dana and Steve look over the map, I quietly ask the clerk one more question about the attached papers. She confirms my suspicion. I ask Dana if she knows how to get there.

"No worries. Easy peasy," Dana says.

"Come on, fess up. What's this about?" Steve asks as

we head out the door.

I shake my head. He takes the hint.

CHAPTER TWENTY-FOUR

After a long drive on unpaved roads, Dana says, "We're close."

Steve says, "Stop near that bush. According to my GPS, that's the closest we can get in a car."

Dana and Steve confer a moment. Dana points off the road across the desert, toward a series of escarpments and plateaus. "Over in that direction. Near where that dip is and the land starts to rise."

Steve agrees, "We'll have to walk."

I park our SUV.

Good thing we followed Dana's suggestion and went back to our rooms for boots and water before leaving town.

We hike in, watching carefully where we place our feet for snakes and other critters. Steve leads, following his cell phone's GPS.

We near a pile of rocks. An animal jumps out, startling

me. Whew. It's only a wallaby, a medium sized type of kangaroo. Our approach must have woken the wallaby from a nap in the shade of the rocks. It passes us as it departs rapidly in a series of ground covering leaps. It disappears over a low ridge.

I force myself to relax. I didn't realize how tense I am.

"We're close," Steve says. "But not good. I just lost all bars on my phone. No calls from here on."

Dana and I check our phones. We're out of coverage, too. I should have brought a sat phone, but never thought I'd need one on this trip.

"GPS still working?" I ask.

"No," he says. "I estimate that Ted's land is right over there, though."

We trudge toward the base of the escarpment.

"This is the area," says Steve. "What are we looking for?"

We look around. Nothing -- for miles. We can't even see our SUV back at the road because of the slight roll to the ground.

"Why on earth would Ted buy a property this far out of town?" asks Dana.

I had an idea, but now I'm doubting it. Looking around, the area looks untouched. Walking a little further, I notice a couple scraggly trees where the ground has a bit of a dip on the far side. I head in that direction. Dana and Steve trail along behind.

"Be careful where you walk," I say.

"Those are Kurkara trees," Dana points them out.

I reach the trees and stop. Steve and Dana join me.

"That's what I was looking for." I point to a four foot diameter shaft hidden from casual view by the trees. "Is that a mine?"

"Looks like it," says Dana, as she peers down it.

"How did you know that was here?" Asks Steve.

"Dana said one of the pages we found at Willis' is a grant for mining rights."

"There's no pile of excavated dirt. Must not have been worked in quite a while," Dana says.

I walk toward the opening. Stop and kick the surface area. "Look closer. Someone's gone to great lengths to make it appear that way. They've scattered the mine tailings all around the area, so there's no pile to give away that there's a shaft here."

We look down the shaft, but it's too dark to see anything.

"I wonder how deep it is." Steve says.

I pick up a rock and drop it down the shaft. There's a dull thud. "That was about a second and a half," I say. "If I remember right, the rate of a falling object is about thirty-two feet a second, so a guess-timate would be around forty-five, fifty feet."

"Too bad there's no way down," says Dana. "You should go down in one some time."

I leave them by the opening and walk back toward the trees. I examine the area nearby. Spotting a bump in the sand, I nudge it with my foot. Nothing but sand. I spot another raised area and nudge it. More sand.

Curious, Steve and Dana come to watch me.

"What are you doing?" Asks Steve.

"I'm wondering whether someone is working Ted's mine illegally. If that's true, they would probably leave their tools here. That way no one would see them in their car and ask questions. And since this area is rolling and open desert, the best place to hide them would be to bury them."

For the next half hour, we search the immediate area with zero luck. I'm about to call it quits as Steve yells from next to a low rock. "Here."

Dropping to his knees, he digs. By the time Dana and I reach him, he's pulling up a large canvas bag. He shakes off the loose sand and opens the drawstring closure. Inside is a rolled up rope ladder, two long metal stakes and a short sledge hammer.

"That's how they're getting up and down the shaft."

"Cool. Let's do it," Dana says. "This is our chance."

"Do what?" Steve asks.

"Let's take a look. Come on. It'll be fun."

Go down in the mine? "Not necessary," I say. "It's too big a risk."

"You want to know how recently the mine has been worked. This ladder could have been here for ages," Dana says.

Rats. She has a point. "Okay, take a quick look and check that ladder first for dry rot."

The ladder appears to be strong, so we drive the stakes into the ground near the edge of the shaft and secure the loops of the rope ladder over them. The ladder unrolls into the shaft. The lower rungs land at the bottom with a thud. Dana and Steve scramble down with Steve using his phone as a flashlight.

Nothing could entice me into a dark hole in the ground. I wait at the top. All I can think is all that rock and dirt over my head, ready to come down at any second.

"This is neat, Lexi," Steve yells up at me. "Come on down. You'll want to see this. The shaft seems to join a natural cave and it does look like someone's been here recently."

"No thanks. You've been down there long enough. Come back. It's time to go."

I bend over to hear his response better --

Something slams me hard in my back.

Suddenly I'm falling head first down the shaft. My right hand scrapes the rough walls, trying to grab anything that might slow my fall. My sunglasses fall away.

My hand bumps against the ladder. I grab at it with all my strength. My fingers close tightly over the rope. There's an immediate pain in my shoulder as I jerk to a full stop -- clutching the ladder. My other hand quickly joins the first one on the rope. I take a deep breath. Thank goodness. I'm no longer falling head first.

I look down. Fifteen feet more and I would have crashed into the packed earthen floor of the shaft. I shudder and grasp the ladder tighter.

In the silence, I can hear Steve and Dana chatting excitedly off in the adjoining tunnel. I take a deep breath. That was a close one.

I notice a pain in my back where I was hit.

The ladder twitches in my hand. I look up with apprehension. There's only the round view of the blue sky. Then a shadow partially blocks the light.

Someone or something is up there.

One side of the ladder abruptly collapses, no longer hooked over its stake. There's a tremor in the second side. I scramble downward as fast as I can. My feet are still six feet from the bottom when the ladder gives way totally.

I land in a heap as the ladder crashes down on top of me. Everything goes black.

CHAPTER TWENTY-FIVE

"Lexi, Lexi. Wake up." It's Steve as he slaps my face. His voice sounds a hundred miles away.

I slowly open my eyes. His concerned face hovers right over mine. Only he now has four eyes and two noses. Strange.

"Are you all right?"

My eyes close. No, I don't think so. My body hurts. My head is spinning.

"What happened? Did the ladder break?" Dana asks.

"You could say that," comes out of my mouth all garbled.

"She's not making sense," he says. He shakes me harder. I wish he'd stop doing that. It's painful.

A shower of sand and stones rains down on us.

Alarmed, Steve says, "Quick. Help me pull her further into the tunnel."

They drag me away from the shaft just in time.

Kablam! There's a loud explosion. The mine shakes like an earthquake. Rocks and sandstone crash down the shaft. The noise is horrific. The dust engulfs us like a tidal wave.

Followed by an ominous silence.

I shudder as the expression "silent as a grave" crosses my mind. My hearing clears as a single small rock bounces down the edge of the debris filled shaft hitting me in the leg.

Fully conscious now, I lie still, covering my face until the dust clears. Forcing myself to a sitting position, I see Dana braced against the wall beside me, coughing and clutching Steve's phone, still on in flashlight mode.

Feeling woozy, I look around for Steve. He's sprawled face down among the rocks and dirt. Motionless.

Alarmed, I crawl toward him. Relief shoots through me when he inhales sharply and vomits dirt.

He's alive.

Dana joins me and shines her light on his face. Near as I can tell in the poor light, his eyes look clear. I check Dana's. Hers look good too.

"I'm okay," she says.

"Steve?"

Still having fits of gagging, he waves his hand to signal he's fine.

Dana helps him sit up and wipes his face with her sleeve.

Thank goodness. I'm overwhelmed with emotion. I

never should have brought them with me. I didn't anticipate any danger, but I should have. Whoever we're looking for has already committed one murder, possibly even two that we know about. Maybe three more if I can't get us out of here.

"What happened?" Steve asks.

"You can tell your father that we left no stone unturned," I say.

Steve manages a weak smile.

Dana looks at me like I'm crazy. She might not be too far off. My brain isn't working at a hundred percent.

"The mine shaft caved in after Lexi fell," Dana says.

"Not caved in," I correct. "It was blown up."

Their faces reflect their shock as they absorb this.

"Why would anyone..."

"Later. First things first."

Using the cave's side wall for balance, I stand. My legs wobble badly. Time to assess the situation. It can't be good.

I swallow my fear, take a deep breath, and remove my cell phone from my pocket. Drat. It was a crazy hope, but still no service this deep underground. Steve checks his. Same thing.

"Mine's out of range, too." Dana says.

Not good. There's no way we can call for help. This might be one time I'd be happy to see the police. The SUV has GPS. The rental company might eventually look for it, but the earliest would be after next week. I took the two week rental special. My spirits take another nose dive. The police and the car company will think the car was abandoned. There's no reason for them to imagine we're trapped down here.

Our situation is critical.

I turn my flashlight app on as I stagger to the pile of rubble that fills the shaft. Things are not looking good. The entire shaft area is filled. Trying to dig up through fifty feet of dirt and rocks with our bare hands would be futile.

Dana and Steve move beside me. No one says a word. This is all my fault. I should never have let the kids enter the mine.

Finally breaking the silence, Steve points at the cave in. "Look at that," he says with surprise. He reaches into the dirt and pulls out a large piece of rough opal. "It's like the one in your ring."

I turn my light on it. If it were polished, it would match my new ring perfectly. My hunch was right. Riley must be secretly mining Ted's property.

I'm about to share my theory about Riley with Steve when I notice something odd sticking out of edge of the rubble. I move closer and gasp.

It's a human.

I fall on my knees and dig frantically. Steve and Dana join me. In seconds we unearth Riley's head and shoulders. He's face down and not breathing.

"What's he doing here?" Steve asks.

"Nothing good," I say. Joan must have told him where we were headed. Apparently Riley knew exactly where the property is located even though Joan didn't.

I give him a whack on his back, not sure what do in a situation like this. We manage to drag him clear and turn him over. I immediately start CPR. Nothing.

After a bit, Steve pushes me aside and takes over.

We're about to give up when Riley suddenly gasps. His eyes open for a split second and then close. His breathing continues raggedly. Still, it's amazing that he's survived at all.

"Riley, are you okay?" No response.

"Is he okay?" asks Dana. "There's a huge lump on his head. Maybe he has a concussion. I heard about a guy who got amnesia from a bump like that. Lost his memory completely."

Riley's eyelids flutter again. I check him over. Since there are no obvious other injuries, I give him a sharp poke. "Riley, wake up."

He groans.

I poke him harder. "Come on, Riley, you need to tell us. Do you hurt anywhere?"

His eyes pop open. "Where am I?"

I'm blown away that he's coherent after what his body's been through. If he was a cat, he just used up all nine of his lives plus a few extra ones. But I don't believe he's lost his memory. It's just way too convenient an out for him. And drat Dana for suggesting a way for him to avoid answering questions. I shoot a look of disbelief at Steve.

He nods, getting my message.

Dana says, "You were in a cave in. Do you remember?"

The better question, I think, is why are you here.

Riley sits up with an assist from Dana. "In a cave? Who are you people? Where am I?"

I can't help myself. My eyes roll.

Dana appears to buy the amnesia totally. "We're friends," she says. "Where does it hurt?"

Riley groans.

"You're safe for now. We just need to figure a way out of here and get you to a hospital." She gives him a sip from her water bottle.

The police station would be a better place. I guess now's not the time to mention that.

"Let's preserve the phone batteries. We may need the lights later," I say.

I motion to Steve to watch Riley and return my attention to the shaft. I turn my phone light on and scan it over the area.

Exactly as I thought. Not good. The shaft is packed. There's no way to tell how much rubble is between us and the surface above. Although my best estimate is too much.

How did Riley manage to get caught in his own trap? The only way a cave in like this could have happened is if he dynamited the shaft. Maybe it went off prematurely before he could move far enough away.

I double check my cell phone. Still no reception. And I didn't tell anyone where we were going. All Joan knows is we went to see her property. I didn't tell her where it was. Andre won't be back until later. He'll know we're missing, but won't have a clue where.

I try to think. This is bad. I can hear Dana chatting with Riley nearby as I slide down into a sitting position.

What have I heard about people stuck in tunnels? The first thing is air. We're still coughing, but now that the dust is settling, the air seems okay. If this is a big tunnel, there must be a lot of oxygen inside it. Enough at least not to be an immediate concern.

The thought of the millions of tons of earth and rock above us makes me nauseous.

Steve slides next to me and says, "We could die down here, couldn't we?"

I make an effort to pull myself together. "Let's not plan on that. We can try to dig our way our through the shaft, but I hope that's our last resort."

"What then? Look for another entrance?"

"That has its own risks, but may be our best chance."

"If there is another entrance, it could be miles away, or the tunnel has lots of branches or it's caved in between us and the entrance. We could get lost."

A mentor once told me, "if you're overwhelmed, focus on the practical and concentrate on what you can do.

Ignore the rest." It's advice I've always followed. I struggle to hide my own anxiety. "Let's not create more obstacles than we already have," I say.

"But Riley's injured. We can't leave him."

I can hear Dana questioning Riley about his injuries. Riley murmurs his responses.

I lower my voice. "I think Riley killed Ted to steal this mine. Judging by the price of my ring and Neddy saying black opals are rare in Coober Pedy, this mine must be worth a fortune. Maybe way more than the three million Ted embezzled. And if Riley marries Joan, he'll own it."

Steve stifles a gasp.

We both involuntarily glance where Dana and Riley continue to talk.

A thought strikes me. Riley must know if there is a second entrance. It's probably the way he or Ted entered originally before digging the shaft.

I whisper to Steve, "If Riley's faking amnesia, he may manage to bolt. Try to stay between him and the tunnel. I don't want him to give us the slip and leave us here."

Steve pauses a second, then scrambles to his feet. He casually moves into position past Riley.

I like that Steve doesn't ask questions. He absorbs and reacts. He has a good future ahead of him as an investigator if...and it's a big if at this point...I can get us out of here alive.

I approach Dana and Riley. Steve holds his position

between Riley and the deeper tunnel.

"Nobody's going to find us here," I say. "Our best option may be to see if the tunnel has another entrance while we have water and energy. Riley, do you think you can stand?"

"Am I Riley?" he asks.

"Yes, that's your name," says Dana. "I'm Dana. Come on. I'll help you."

Leaning heavily on her, he manages to stand upright.

"Think you can walk?"

He staggers a few weak steps with Dana's help, gathering a little strength as he goes. He's not a hundred percent steady on his feet, but that's good. It will make it more difficult for him to give us the slip.

We check our water supplies. There's about twenty-four ounces between us.

"Riley, do you have a phone? We'll need light."

He shrugs. Before he can react, Dana pats his pockets, discovers he does, and lifts it out. She hands it to me.

"Let's go then. I'll lead, then Riley and Dana. Steve, you bring up the rear. Only one light on at a time. We'll need to conserve," I say, trying to appear confident. "Speak up if you need to stop."

With a shudder to swallow my own fears, we set off into the unknown tunnel. I'm no longer scared. I'm terrified.

CHAPTER TWENTY-SIX

We move through the cave in silence. It seems like forever, but it's only been an hour plus. We've stopped twice already in that time for Riley to rest.

Its elevation seems to go up and down. The ceiling seems to range from four to twenty feet above us. At the low sections, we've been forced to crawl over the sharp rocks and debris scattered on the floor. When the ceiling allows, we stand and walk carefully. The good thing is we've seen no branches off the tunnel, so we haven't had to make any directional choices. Since the mining here has been for opals which only appears in a layer between sandstone and clay, there probably aren't any downward vertical shafts like other mines. But we still have to be alert for natural sinkholes and crevasses. The air is stale, but breathable.

"I need to stop," Riley says.

"I could use a drink," says Dana.

I do a quick scan of the area before turning off the light to conserve the battery as we rest. Sitting still isn't good for me. My body stiffens as my imagination returns to the weight of all the rocks and dirt above us. I shudder, forcing myself to think of something good -- Andre. How I love joking with him. How the thought of him lifts my spirits. How attractive he is. Followed by how can I ever trust him? Will I ever see him again?

My thoughts are interrupted by the sounds of a scuffle and a curse from Riley. I snap on the light.

Riley lies face down with Steve clutching his leg.

Steve and I exchange a look. Riley was trying to get away.

Steve helps Riley up. "Sorry, Riley. You tripped over my foot."

Riley glances around at our faces. "Just wanted to take a piss."

Sure you did, I think. But I say, "Let Steve help you. Otherwise you might have another fall. Come on, we better start moving again." I wish I could ask him how much further we have to go. Of course, I'm sure he'll pretend he has no idea.

We walk on with Steve staying close to Riley. I realize Riley may not make it much further. He's becoming more and more uncoordinated. He was lucky. He could have easily been killed in the explosion.

I take a deep breath, The air feels fresher. We round a bend to see a faint light ahead. I turn off the cell phone and we can still see. Now if only there's an entrance large enough we can escape through. I tell myself that Ted must have got into the cave before the mine shaft was dug. Hopefully that means we can get out.

I'm emotionally overwhelmed when we turn the next corner of the cave and light pours in through a large crevasse.

***

It's early evening as we emerge from the tunnel. Steve and I exchange a quick high-five. We're out. Definitely a moment of pure joy. I notice Dana is smiling, but Riley appears apprehensive.

Riley seems nice. Am I right to suspect him? It's hard to believe he's responsible for so much grief and Ted's death.

I look around, trying to gage our location. After a few moments, I realize we're on the far side of the escarpment that was behind the mine shaft. We'll need to hike around the end of the escarpment and pass the original mine shaft to reach our SUV and the road.

We're exhausted emotionally and physically. Still, the next hour of walking goes with lighter hearts. It's dark by the time we finally reach Ted's mine shaft that we'd originally entered. Or rather, what's left of it.

With the use of the cell phone lights, we can see that

only a shallow concave depression remains. Rocks, sandstone, and debris have filled the shaft all the way to the surface. Thank goodness we didn't try to dig out. We would never have made it. There's an involuntary moment of silence as we realize we could still be down there...or dead.

No one would ever know. All traces of our earlier presence are gone.

We drag ourselves toward the road. Thoughts of a shower, clean clothes, dinner...and Andre fill my head.

Steve comes up beside me. "What about Riley?" He whispers.

"Nothing we can do now. We'll talk at the hotel."

Moments later we reach the road. Even though it's night, I realize I can't see the outline of our SUV. I'm stunned and quickly turn on the cell phone light.

No mistake. The SUV is gone. Car thieves? How can that be out here in the boonies?

Steve and Dana ask in unison, "Where's the car?"

I shine the light to the left. Empty road. I swing the light to the right. There, about half a mile away, is darker area the size and shape of a vehicle.

"Looks like you forgot to set the brake," Dana says sarcastically.

Could the brake have released and the SUV rolled away? No. The ground is almost level here. I ignore Dana and head toward it. The group follows.

As we approach, our flashlights reveal an old ute. Riley's ute. I hadn't thought about it, but of course he had to arrive here somehow. I scan the area again with the light. Nothing, but a deserted road in a dark, empty desert. Where is our SUV?

I tell myself I'll worry about it later. "Riley, This is your truck. Do you remember it?"

He shakes his head.

"Looks like you're our transportation. Hand me your keys, will you. We'll get you to the closest doctor."

"I don't need a doctor. I can drive."

"Your memory's back?"

"Uh, well no."

"Not a good idea to drive with amnesia. Better if I do."

Reluctantly Riley hands over the keys.

"Okay. Everybody in." The truck has a bench seat and we all manage to squeeze in. Riley slowly pulls himself in last and shuts the passenger door.

"I'm truly glad to be going home," Dana says.

Me, too. For a while there I wasn't sure we'd make it. I start up the ute, shift it into gear, and we head back toward Coober Pedy.

There's silence for a while, broken only by the noise of the tires on the dirt road.

Suddenly Dana yells, "I've got reception!" She dials furiously. "Dad, it's me...I'm okay...I'll be home in a bit...It's complicated. I'm with the Harrisons and Riley

Pettersen...Yea, she took us to this cave and it fell in..."

I, and anyone else in a two mile radius, can hear her father yelling loud and clear. "Lexi is a stupid Shelia." He'll have my hide for letting Dana go into a mine.

Dana cuts him off. "I'll tell her. See you in a jif." She turns to me. "Lexi, Dad says Andre's hunting for you. You didn't tell him where we were going either."

Steve interrupts, "Dana, that's not fair."

She gives him a hard look.

"Your father's right," I say. "I should have never let either of you go down in the mine."

Silence.

I don't have a phone number for Andre. He'll have to wait until we're back to town. Still, I do have a question for Riley. "How did you manage to find us today?"

"I found you? I don't remember."

Right. "Which way to the closest doctor?" I ask Dana.

"When you get to the paved road," she says. "Turn like we're headed back to town."

After we've driven another few minutes on the dirt road, I notice a vehicle hurtling toward us. It has such a big dust cloud trailing behind it that I almost don't recognize Andre's Land Cruiser until he's passing us.

I lay on the horn and blink the headlights. He stops in a hard skid. He jumps out and races on foot back to the truck.

I jump out to meet him. His arms wrap around me.

They never felt so good.

"Thank goodness, Cherie," he says. "I was afraid something happened to you. Where were you?"

I whisper, "Not now, big news later." Louder I say, "Riley's hurt. We need to take him to a doctor."

Andre squeezes me again. "Is he all right?"

"Memory loss. We need to hurry."

"Okay, I'll follow you." He rushes to his vehicle and turns in behind us.

I start the truck and head for town.

Steve's phone rings. He looks at the screen. With a laugh, cancels the call. We exchange a quick look. "Skylar, from the baseball game," he says. He and I both laugh as Dana and Riley look at us as if we're demented.

CHAPTER TWENTY-SEVEN

Andre listens intently as I tell the doctor that Riley was in a mine cave-in and has amnesia. Riley squirms in his seat as the doctor examines him.

Done, the doctor takes a hard look at me. His eyes linger on my fading black eye, and then to the recent cuts and bruises visible on my arms from the cave-in. "Are you okay?" He asks. "That's a nasty eye."

"I'm okay. The eye is old. The other stuff just needs a good wash." Rats, I think. I need another pair of sunglasses.

He gives Andre a hard look.

"Hey, not me," Andre says. "She says a door ran into her."

Like everybody else, the doctor's not believing a word, but he points out the waiting room to us and leads Riley away for more tests.

The last thing I hear is Riley saying is, "Hey Doc, have

you heard the one about the koala --?" Maybe Riley's been hit in the head too many times before. The door closes behind them and cuts Riley off. Thank goodness.

Steve's already gone. He left in Riley's ute to drive Dana home.

The small waiting room is packed with people from the Prospector's Festival waiting to be seen or waiting for friends or relatives who are being seen.

Andre and I manage to find a corner with two empty chairs. I'm exhausted, and it's all I can do to stay awake.

"Did you learn anything in Lightning Ridge?"

"Only that Riley seems to spend a lot of time up there. Sells a lot of opals to different dealers. What happened here?" he says, keeping his voice low.

"When we saw you on the road earlier, how did you know to look for us out in that direction?"

"Dana's father said he hadn't seen you since you all left in your SUV around lunch time. I went back to my car. Then I spotted your SUV in the far corner of the parking lot.

"It's at the hotel?"

He nods. "I opened the driver's door and saw the keys on floor mat. I found your purse under the seat. That's why I knew you were in trouble."

"How could the car get all the way back to town? I parked it near where we found the mine."

"What mine is this?"

"Tell you in a minute."

"Well, I tried to find you. Dana's father had already been phoning her with no success. He said he called friends and no one had seen any of you in town since early this afternoon. I checked your SUV's GPS system. It told me the last place you'd been parked for a while. I was headed out to that point to see if there was a clue to pick up your trail. Now what's this about a mine?"

"Remember that your friend, Neddy, told us he bought the opal in my ring from Riley?"

He nods.

"While we were shopping this morning, we met a friend of Dana's who was selling a similar opal. He also bought it from Riley. That got me thinking about the paperwork we recovered from Ted's house in California. I called home to the bank and confirmed part of it was Australia's equivalent of a deed with mineral rights. I asked Joan, but she didn't know anything about it. We got directions to go take a look. Sure enough we found a hidden mine. And the opals there are similar to the one in my ring." I went on to describe the cave-in and Riley's arrival.

"He followed you, tried to bury you, but got caught in his own explosion? How nuts is that?" Andre says harshly.

Heads turn in our direction.

"Shh - I think it's possible he had a partner with him that decided they didn't need Riley any longer and shoved him in."

"That's pretty cold-blooded."

"If Riley and his partner had their way, you wouldn't have seen anything or even known there was a mine there or realized we were buried in it."

"I'd guess the partner must have driven your SUV back to town."

"The question is who?"

Andre shakes his head. "Regardless of who his mysterious partner is, I'm struggling to understand how he could steal from Ted and Joan for the last couple years. Then try to kill you, the boy, and Dana? I don't know the guy well, but I'd never have thought him capable of this. And he has the gall to try and marry Joan?"

"Ted's house was searched at the time he was killed and again afterwards. What if that was Riley? What if he didn't know about the three million dollars that Ted embezzled for Joan's hospital bills? What if he was looking for the deed with the mining rights to Ted's mine? Not the money."

"That's a really big 'what if.' Where's the deed now?"

"The original's safe at the bank."

"Keep it there. This is going to break Joan's heart."

"If he married Joan, he'd get the mine legally. Maybe that's his backup plan. Think about it. There's no way Riley could allow Ted to come home. Ted would have discovered someone was working his mine as soon as he went to see it. Even if Ted couldn't prove the thief was Riley, Riley wouldn't be able to steal any longer. His illicit income would have been cut off."

"Riley murdered his closest friend, Ted? That's hard to accept."

"I don't know. I think it's a distinct possibility."

"I'm not sure what to do next."

"We don't know anyone's alibi for the time Ted was killed."

"Maybe we should find out."

"We can't do it without police help to confirm the alibis. Even if we could prove anything, we'd be the ones arrested if we go to them."

His expression hardens. "Don't worry about it. We won't need the police. I can deal with Riley. He'll wish it was the police."

"I'll bet he's going to be pissed with whoever decided he was a liability and shoved him down the mine shaft."

"Who's your best guess? Kenneth? Clare?"

I shrug. "Whoever it is won't be happy to learn that we survived. I think we don't let Riley know we're on to him until we have more information."

"I wouldn't mind beating it out of him."

"Not helpful."

We look up as Riley's doctor enters and approaches us. "Riley appears to have recovered most of his memory except for the last few hours. I'm holding him overnight for observation."

"Please let him know we'll bring his ute back in the morning and pick him up," I say.

The doctor hurries away.

The 1812 Overture rings from my phone. Steve's back in the parking lot.

"We'll be right out," I say.

I make a quick detour on the way through the hospital gift shop for a new pair of sunglasses.

CHAPTER TWENTY-EIGHT

Andre and I reach the parking lot and find Steve beaming ear to ear. He's practically bouncing from foot to foot as he holds up a large boot sized box.

"What?" I ask.

"Guess what I found behind the seat in Riley's ute." He whips the top off the box. It's packed solid with rough opals. I can tell by the colors that they match the ones from Ted's mine. A couple of them are huge. As black opals, they must be worth a fortune.

"Wow!" is all I can manage to say.

"Are those from Ted's mine? They belong to Joan," says Andre angrily.

"We can return them later." I replace the cover on the box. "Let's go back to the hotel and have these put in a safe. Did you find anything else?"

"I stopped after I found these."

"What a smart idea to search the truck," I add.

Steve smiles, pleased.

Andre says "Let's see what else we can find. I only wish we could know who Riley calls after we leave."

"Wait a minute." I pull Riley's phone from my pocket and hold it up. "He can't call anyone unless he uses the hospital phone. I have his."

I remove my cell out of my other pocket. Turning both on, I hold them together for a bit. "I bought one of those new spy apps. I can hack his phone. We can see exactly who he calls as well as his past call list."

"Cool. I want one of those," says Steve.

"On the internet," I say.

Done, I hand Riley's phone to Andre. "Can you return that to him and we'll see who he calls?"

***

Once Andre's back from giving Riley his phone, Steve drives Riley's ute to the first secluded spot he reaches. Andre and I follow right behind in the Land Cruiser.

Steve chooses to sit on a nearby rock and oversee my cell phone. He waits for Riley to make a call. Andre and I search the ute.

"I have a thought," I say. "If the black opals from Ted's mine are rare for this area, and more commonly found at Lightning Ridge, wouldn't it be smart of Riley to sell them where black opals weren't unusual?"

"Makes sense to me," Andre says.

I hold my nose as I remove a pile of filthy work clothes,

followed by a case of empty beer cans. Andre finds a take-out box with mold growing on the food inside. There are a couple of rock picks, a bucket, a crow bar, safety glasses, and a pair of heavily worn work gloves.

"Ugh," I say as I hold up half a roll of toilet paper -- thankfully unused.

A dirty bandana, a half-empty bottle of sunscreen, two maps of the area, and a first aid kit complete our finds. Nothing to help us. Nothing that points to the identity of his partner. Bummer.

I was hoping to find a receipt for airfare to Los Angeles or a hotel bill. Anything that would prove Riley had been in Los Angeles last week.

Disappointed, we shove everything back in the truck, hopefully in the same places we found them.

"Wait a minute," says Andre. He grabs a wrench from his vehicle's tool kit and slides under his Land Cruiser on the side facing away from Steve. There's banging and the noise of the wrench being used, plus a few choice words as dirt and sand drop on his head. Moments later he pushes himself back out.

In his hands is a sealed metal box about a foot square and six plus inches deep. He shakes the dirt out of his hair and opens it.

The inside is packed.

I catch a glimpse of large rubber-banded stacks of currency from multiple countries, a serious Swiss army knife and several passports and identity papers. Four or five credit cards in different names. Plus two guns.

He draws out the weapons, sticks one in his waistband, and hands the other to me. "You better carry this. You're under dressed."

It's a nice Beretta 92FS. The fifteen round model with a reversible magazine and the non-reflective black finish. Basic black and goes with everything. I don't love guns, but it feels good to have one under the circumstances.

"It's loaded and ready to go."

"Wait," says Steve. "Don't I get one?"

"No," Andre and I say simultaneously.

With that, Andre slides back under the vehicle to re-attach the box. A few more minutes and he slides back out.

"What else is under there?" I ask. "The kitchen sink?"

"This and that for emergencies. Derain takes care of my Cruiser. He and I made a few modifications. It has a double petrol tank, and the tires are puncture proof. A flat can be a really bad thing if you're running from the police or people worse than the police."

No wonder the bumps from riding in his car felt extremely hard.

It's late and Steve and I are exhausted. We call it a night. Steve reports that Riley hasn't made any calls. Time to head for the hotel.

Since Steve and I missed our flight earlier tonight, I'll need to rebook us for tomorrow.

CHAPTER TWENTY-NINE

"Stay away from my daughter," Dana's father, Tom, growls. "And I want you checking out of my hotel first thing tomorrow morning."

"Really, Tom," says Andre. "Isn't that a bit extreme?"

"Not after Dana explained today's happenings. She would never have been in that cave-in if she hadn't been talked into it."

"But she's fine," says Andre.

"No thanks to your friends."

I'm not sure why Andre's arguing. Steve and I are checking out tomorrow anyway. I'm too exhausted to get involved. I can see this day's exertion has caught up with Steve, too. He's collapsed in a lobby chair, still clutching the box of opals. Much as I'd like to put them in the hotel safe, I don't see that happening now since Tom's so mad.

Tom eventually finishes his diatribe and we head for our rooms. Andre follows.

I stop him. "Where are you going?"

"With you. It may not be safe. Remember the snake? Whoever's behind this knows where you're staying."

Good point. I turn to Steve. "Maybe it would be better if we sleep in your room tonight."

Andre scowls.

"He shouldn't be alone either and it might be safer than my room," I say to him.

"We won't need you," Steve says to Andre. "I can protect Lexi."

"Yeh. Like you've been doing a bloody bang up job of it so far."

"At least I didn't disappear for over a year."

"It wasn't by choice."

Wouldn't I like to hear the answer to that, I think. But not tonight.

"Knock it off both of you," I say. "Check the room's clear first and Steve, keep those opals close. Let me collect my things and I'll be back."

***

After a quick shower, I pack my things and carry them to Steve's room. I open the door, and I'd laugh if I had the energy.

There are two double beds in the room. Andre has commandeered one and Steve the other. Andre pats the bed beside him invitingly. Steve's rolled to the far side of his bed to show how much room there is as they attempt to make me choose between them.

First I take a towel from the bathroom and wedge it under the door. No snakes tonight. Grabbing the comforter from Steve's bed and a pillow from Andre's, I use them to make a bed on the floor.

Andre and Steve protest.

"Enough," I say. "Goodnight." I'm asleep in minutes.

CHAPTER THIRTY

Last night was a rough one for me. One recurring dream terrified me. In it, I wandered alone through an endless tunnel in the dark, stumbling and calling out. The only thing I could hear were the echoes of my own cries. Doesn't take a psychiatrist to explain that one.

If I wasn't starving, I'd wish we hadn't come to the restaurant for breakfast. It's packed with happy, costumed festival attendees. All talking at the top of their voices. It takes me a minute to remember today is opening day of events. Costume judging, camel rides, cook offs, horse racing, and a golf tournament. I don't think prospectors pursued a lot of golf way back then, but who am I to quibble. Maybe they brought their golf clubs with them just in case.

Today's our last day here. We had to buy new tickets, since we missed last night's plane. In a few more hours Steve and I will be flying home. I sip my coffee and gently shift the heavy tote bag on my lap that now contains the rough opals Steve found in Riley's ute. Andre checks out the menu. Steve punches numbers in my phone, still watching for Riley to make a call. The only one he made last night was to Joan's number. We haven't spoken to each other since we got up this morning and I bring them up to speed.

"I bought tickets this morning for us to go home this afternoon," I announce.

Steve says, "But we haven't solved the case."

Andre looks stunned. "Cherie...?"

The only thing unsolved for me is Andre. I realize now how much I love him, but where do we go from here? I still don't know what his feelings are for me. Can I trust what he tells me?

"I need to get Steve away from here," I say. "Someone is trying to kill us. Next time they could succeed. There is no logical reason for either of us to stay one minute longer."

Steve tries to interrupt, but I cut him off. "The money Ted stole is gone. There's no way it's recoverable without it being a death sentence for Joan. We agreed not to do that."

"Right," says Steve.

I try not to think about losing my job. "We can give Joan the facts about the mine and Riley's thefts after we drop his ute off at the hospital. What she does with the knowledge is up to her. End of story. Much as I'd like to, there's no need for us to discover the identity of Riley's partner. That's not why we're here. Since that's the situation, we're going home."

In the middle of all the hubbub circling us from enthusiastic festival goers, the three of us are mute. The waitress gives us a funny look as she refills our coffee. She breaks the silence by asking for our order. Suddenly I'm not hungry anymore.

I cut off any arguments from Steve. It's the pain on Andre's face that punctures my heart. Still, I know I'm right. Steve won't leave if I don't go with him. His safety has to come before my desire to stay with Andre. Steve and I have already lingered here too long.

Steve breaks the silence. "I wrote out a list of numbers Riley called in the last month. We can look at them."

Andre checks through the numbers as we eat. I pull up the ones he doesn't recognize from a reverse phone directory. Other than multiple ones to Joan, the rest are to various opal stores, and to dealers in Lightning Ridge.

No useful calls so far to point us toward Riley's partner.

Done with breakfast, we head back to the hotel parking lot, where we're met with new troubles.

The tire slasher has returned for an encore. The tires on Riley's truck and our SUV are slashed. Only the tires on Andre's Land Cruiser are okay even though they have slash marks on them. At least they're not flat. In addition, all three vehicles have been vandalized. Driver's side windows are smashed. Doors gape open. The contents of Riley's ute are strewn about. The meager contents of Steve's and my bags are dumped on the ground and blowing across the parking lot. The vehicles were fine before we left for breakfast. All this happened in the short time we were eating.

Andre swears. Steve is speechless. I look around. The slasher can't be too far away. We weren't at breakfast that long.

The car rental company is going to have a fit, is my second thought.

Andre turns to face me. "Someone really doesn't like you."

"What do you think they were looking for?" Steve asks.

"The opals," Andre and I say in unison.

Thank goodness I had the opals with me. "Who even knew there were opals?"

"Riley's in the hospital," Andre says. "Has to be his partner."

He slides under his Land Cruiser, and says, "Looks like everything's okay under here."

I nod and start grabbing clothes from around the pavement with Steve. He and I pile all our loose clothes on the back seat of the SUV.

Andre heads inside to see if Tom or Dana witnessed the destruction as I try to pack the contents of Riley's ute into their original places again.

I turn to Steve. "Better call Riley and tell him what's happened to his truck and that we're going to be late."

It feels weird replacing the contents of Riley's ute again. At least I can remember where most of the stuff goes.

I hear Steve ask the hospital for Riley's room, then he's silent.

"Lexi?" Says Steve in a low voice. "Riley didn't answer his cell so I called the hospital..."

"Yes?"

"He checked out last night."

"What?"

"Right after we left."

"I was so tired last night it never occurred to me he would do that," I say.

"Then it's possible he trashed the cars himself this morning. And now he knows we found the opals."

"Highly unlikely he would have trashed his own ute and slashed his own tires."

Andre joins us in the hotel parking lot. "Dana and Tom had a busy morning and didn't hear or see a thing."

I fill him in on Riley's departure from the hospital.

"Let's take my car and head for Joan's. We can bring her up to speed, and drop off the opals," he says. "We'll deal with the rest later. Was anything missing?"

"No," says Steve.

I think a minute and realize, "Yes."

They both look at me.

"The pendant I bought for my mother yesterday. The one with an opal that matches my ring. The opal earrings I got at the same time for my sister are here, but not the pendant."

"Definitely looking for the black opals from Ted's mine."

"You think the partner and the tire slasher are the same?" Steve asks.

"Looks that way. Where does Riley live?" I ask.

"Out by the Lassiter's," Andre says.

"I'd like to stop by there on the way."

CHAPTER THIRTY-ONE

Half an hour later, Andre stops his car in front of Riley's house.

It's a rundown place that sits by itself in a desolate area. All colors have been baked by the sun to a bland beige color. Mini wind vortexes blow sand across the yard past old tires and stacks of broken boards. There's the hum of a generator.

What a sad place, I think.

The three of us exit the Land Cruiser.

Andre bangs on the door. "Hey, Riley, it's Andre. We have --"

Eerily, the door swings open from the force of Andre's knocking.

Silence.

We exchange nervous looks. Andre and I instinctively draw our guns while exchanging nervous looks. I signal Steve to stay back. This can't be good.

"Maybe he stayed in town with friends last night," says Steve.

And left his door open? Not likely. Unclosed and unlocked doors make me uneasy. We enter slowly.

Inside is nothing like I expected. I pause to look around. As decrepit as the exterior of the house appears, the interior is ultra luxurious. A huge flat screen television takes up most of one living room wall. The floors are polished wood. The furniture modern and comfortable. A stack of unopened cartons sits in a corner. The biggest surprise is the coolness of the inside temperature. The cooling system alone must have cost a fortune this far from any power lines.

Andre calls out Riley's name again as I wander down the hall toward the bedroom. All the bedding is top of the line brands. I flip through Riley's clothes in the closet. Suits and shirts. Again, all with high end designer names like Armani and Tom Ford. I spot three pair of expensive, handmade leather boots.

Did Andre made a mistake and this isn't Riley's place? Or has Riley been stealing from Ted's mine for a long time?

"Lexi," Andre calls.

I join Andre and Steve at the door to the kitchen. A glance inside reveals the latest in high-end appliances on the counters.

A perfect cook's kitchen. Except for one thing - poor Riley spread-eagled on the floor with a bullet hole in the center of his forehead.

I check Riley's pulse. Sadly, there isn't one. I shake my head to confirm what the others already know. A dead end. Without Riley, where can we go from here?

Andre says, "We need to get out of here fast. Wipe anything you've touched. Hurry."

"What's the rush?" Steve asks.

"Just do it." I tell him. "We can't afford to be implicated in Riley's death or involved with the police."

We're out of the house, in the Land Cruiser, and back on the road in seven minutes flat.

"Once his body is found, the police will discover he was in the hospital yesterday...with us," Andre says.

"The hospital has CCTV," I say.

In the distance, there's the wail of a police siren headed in our direction.

"The police? Already?" Steve says.

"Anyone think Riley's partner watched for us to arrive and then called the police?" I ask.

Andre drives off the road where there's a depression deep enough to hide the Land Cruiser and stops. We hold our breath that we're not spotted.

It's only moments later that a lone police car speeds past our hiding place. The second it's out of sight, Andre reverses onto the road heading back toward Coober Pedy and floors the gas pedal.

"We need to leave Australia now, by the fastest means

possible" I say.

CHAPTER THIRTY-TWO

It's late morning by the time we're back in Coober Pedy, Andre parks his Land Cruiser as Steve and I grab our stuff from our SUV, including our fly hats.

Dana runs out of the hotel with Steve's boomerang. "Here," she says. "You forgot this."

Steve mumbles something, and she kisses him on the cheek before running back inside.

I decide to run in to use the loo and agree to meet Steve and Andre down the block at the local convenience store. They'll stock us up with gas, food and water we'll need before leaving here.

Minutes later, I'm hurrying down the crowded sidewalk, anxious to get going and leave town. The flies are out so I quickly jam my fly hat on my head.

Suddenly I'm grabbed from behind and spun around.

Time stops. I'm facing my worst nightmare. Ian Brode. The Detective Inspector from Sydney.

He snatches my hat off. The smile on his face isn't a pleasant one.

"Miss Winslow," he hisses. "How nice to see you again."

His tongue flicks, reminding me of the snake in my hotel room. Only Brode might be far more dangerous.

Over his shoulder I see Andre down the block by the Land Cruiser. He spots Brode and pulls Steve out of sight. I blink and they're gone. Thank goodness.

"Cat got your tongue?" Brode asks.

I consider breaking away, but stop. I can't risk having him add "assault on an officer charges" against me.

He increases his pressure on my arm. With his other hand he produces a pair of handcuffs. He jerks my hands behind my back and cuffs them together.

A passing couple pauses and gasps, pointing to the handcuffs.

"Let's take a nice little stroll over to the local cop shop, shall we?" He drags me toward the police station a few blocks away. "You do remember what I said would happen if you ever set foot in Australia again?"

I swallow. My mouth is suddenly dry. It's hard for me to hear over the blacksmith's hammer pounding in my heart. This is it? I'm going to prison? I stumble, but his grip only tightens.

"This isn't right," I say. "Let me go. You know I haven't done anything."

"You did plenty. I was demoted for not being able to charge you. Don't worry about the charges this time. I'll find some good ones."

He would really do that? Arrest me and make something up? What kind of policeman is he?

"How did you know I was here?" I ask.

"From a tip call yesterday. I tracked your flight to Adelaide and then lost you."

Riley's partner has been busy.

"Where's Van der Meer?

"Right here, Brode," Andre says.

The crowd of people watching us gasps and backs away.

Brode jerks me to a halt. I look ahead where he's focused.

It's Andre. He stands on the sidewalk about fifteen feet in front of us.

"Let her go," he says. "It's me you really want."

The crowd, fearing a fight, scurries away in seconds.

I hear one man say, "Hey, it's not real. They must be actors. It's part of a re-enactment for the Prospectors' Festival." Intrigued, people crowd back around us to watch.

Brode stares at Andre with a nasty grin plastered on his face. "Mr. Van der Meer, it's a pleasure to see you. You're taller than you look in your mug shots."

"And you're every bit the drongo I thought you'd be. Let her go, Brode. It's me you want. Release her and you can take me in."

"What's she to you? She claims she wasn't involved."

"She wasn't. I'd hate to see you make more of a flaming galah of yourself than necessary."

Brode tries to push me closer to Andre, but I resist. My resistance makes him angry. Totally focused on Andre, Brode shoves me hard in Andre's direction. Caught off balance with my hands cuffed behind me, I fall to my knees.

Andre's gun appears in his hand, pointing directly at Brode.

"Maybe I just shoot you right here for abuse to women."

"Andre," I plead desperately as I get up. "Run! Run while you can."

He smiles at me. "I wasn't here the last time he abused you. He's not going to do it again."

"You'll never get out of the country," Brode says. "I already have alerts and road blocks out for you."

"I said, let her go and you can take me. I'm laying my gun down."

Andre cares that much he would do that for me?

The crowd tightens around us, listening to every word.

Brode smiles, "I think I'll keep you both." He pulls me in front of him like a shield.

"That's not the deal on the table here. Only me," Andre says.

I can't let this happen because of me. I gather myself to take Brode down when he unexpectedly drags me to the side and approaches Andre.

Brode pulls zip ties from his pocket with his other hand as Andre holds his wrists out.

"Run, Lexi," Andre says. "Get out of here."

Brode clutches me closer.

This can't be happening. Is Andre giving himself up to save me? He would do that? He would go to jail for me? There must be something I can do to stop this. I stand flat-footed and look around the crowd. I spot Steve in the back near Andre's car. But as I watch, he turns without any change of expression and hurries to the Land Cruiser.

Brode grips my arm tighter as he restrains Andre. He pockets Andre's gun.

"Move along, mates. Nothing of interest here," Brode smiles to the crowd. He's actually enjoying having an audience.

The people disperse, laughing and chatting among themselves.

Andre blows me a kiss before Brode spins him around and marches us toward the police station.

Tears roll silently down my face. This can't be the end for us. I can't bear the thought of him in prison on my account.

Suddenly, Brode drops to the ground -- out cold. Andre stares down at him in disbelief.

I look at Brode's doubled up body in surprise. A boomerang lays on the ground beside Brode. Steve did it! He actually did it! I'm never going to laugh at another one of his crazy buys again.

Around us, the remaining crowd erupts in applause. Andre hurries to me and whispers, "Bow."

I do and we take bows as long as the applause continues.

Soon the lingering crowd disperses. Brode's still out cold. Steve appears between the departing crowd and grabs his boomie.

Proudly flipping his Swiss Army knife open, Steve cuts the zip ties on Andre. Andre searches Brode's pockets, removes both guns and the key for my handcuffs. Unlocking the cuffs, he places them on Brode and throws the key as far as he can into the dirt.

I check Brode's pulse. It's strong, He's just out cold with a large red bump developing on his forehead.

"That was impressive," I tell Steve. "Thank you."

"Dana was a good teacher."

"Come," Andre says tersely as he races for his car.

We pile in.

Andre leans over and shakes Steve's hand. "Thanks, Steve. That was a great shot. I owe you."

"You're welcome. But what now?" Steve asks. "How can we get out of the country with the police looking for us? They'll catch us on the road or at the airport."

We look at each other. Nobody has any idea.

"Let's at least leave town while we can," Andre says. The Land Cruiser rattles to life as he steers for the outskirts.

As I look out the window, we pass Penny, my seatmate from the airplane and her friends.

Seconds later, I say, "I have a plan. It might not be the fastest way to go..."

Steve and Andre are skeptical as I outline my idea. I ask, "Anyone have a better idea?" They don't.

Andre makes a quick call. As we reach the edge of town, he slows and turns into the gate at Derain's.

"After my parents died, it was Derain's family that took me in," Andre says. He slows more as we reach the camel paddocks.

Derain is mounting a line of tourists one by one from a mounting block onto a line of saddled camels. A helper leads three more that are saddled out of the barn.

Steve groans, "This is bad. They'll find us here."

"Have some patience," I say.

Andre parks the car behind the hay sheds. He quickly slides under it and retrieves the metal box I saw with his cash and passports. Standing, he says, "Change your clothes so you won't fit Brode's description. Stuff your passports and cash into your pockets. Bring the Beretta. I'll be right back."

He reaches under the seat for the box of Riley's opals

and carries them with his metal box into Derain's house. By the time Steve and I are changed, he returns in tee shirt and jeans carrying three fly hats of a different style and color than the ones we bought at the airport.

"Derain's mom offered these."

We put the new hats on quickly.

Andre hurries back into Derain's house and emerges with a large backpack which appears to contain the contents from his metal box and the box of opals. The backpack must also be courtesy of Derain's mom, too.

"Turn your phones off and take out the SIM cards."

As we do, we follow Andre to the end of the line of tourists being mounted on camels. He steps forward to have a brief word with Derain and quickly returns to the back of the tourist line with Steve and me. While we wait, he makes several rapid calls on his phone. Done, he turns it off and removes his SIM card. Then puts them with ours into a pocket on his backpack.

Steve gives me a questioning look.

"Cross your fingers," I say.

I just hope my plan is a good one, because I'm worried. Really, really worried. The idea of prison overwhelms me. Especially since I'm not guilty of anything. Andre and I are one thing, but I'm responsible for Steve. I'd never forgive myself if he gets caught up in this mess. My plan has to work.

I can feel Steve's nervousness as Derain reaches us and

places him on the third from the last camel. More experienced, Andre and I are quickly mounted on the last two and ready to go.

With a nod, Derain moves away to chat with the tourists. He gives some general instructions before he mounts the lead camel.

With a wave of his arm and a yell, Derain heads the string of camels out the gate.

Moments later, I realize we're headed right back to the center of town. This isn't part of my plan. I panic and twist in the saddle to see Andre. I lift my fly hat to communicate, but he motions immediately for me to pull it down. I see his lips move behind his fly netting. "It's okay."

I do as he says. If I was panicked before, I'm down right horrified now. Especially as Derain turns the camel string right up through the main street of town.

The tourists on the camels ahead of us are waving and yelling to the crowds on the sidewalks. I manage to do a parade wave, hoping to blend in. Steve has the same idea and waves, too. After that, it becomes a bit surreal. Almost like riding a float in a Mardi Gras parade, but without the beads and alcohol. Actually, a little alcohol might be good right now.

The first thing I see are several police stopping people on the sidewalk and asking questions. Nearby, Clare and Kenneth, dressed in prospector costumes, pass out Collins Tour flyers to the crowd.

I hold my breath as we pass the spot where Brode accosted us. At least he's no longer sprawled on the ground where Steve's boomerang left him.

I do spot him on the next block as he approaches a woman with a similar fly hat to my airport one and rips it off her head. She screams. Brode finds himself immediately confronted by the woman's furious husband who punches him. I stifle a laugh. Between that massive punch and Steve's boomerang, Brode's got to have the mother of all headaches.

Through it all, our camels plod forward. Steady and calm. Taking us past all the crowds and festival hubbub. Five minutes later, we're through the town and headed out into the open desert.

I breathe a sigh of relief. Now if Andre can help me make the rest of my plan work.

CHAPTER THIRTY-THREE

Derain leads our camel string out into the desert. The tourists riding in front of us take pictures and talk back and forth happily. Steve, Andre, and I try to blend in, chatting and pretending to laugh. Steve pulls his camera out, too.

We continue on for another hour, passing breathtaking outback views including arid hills, rocky desert, and a surprising number of streams. Eventually we stop for a pre-arranged break in the shade of a small stand of trees. Derain has a mounting block situated here, too. That's smart, I think. Getting on and off camels can be risky because of how much they pitch back and forth when getting up.

Derain helps the tourists down to stretch their legs. He places water and snacks out, then he joins us.

"Thank you, Derain," we say.

He nods, clasping Andre's hand, "No wuckas. Anything for a mate."

They step away to have a private discussion. It annoys me not to hear what Derain is saying. I can tell that he trusts Andre and vice versa.

"What does no wuckas mean?" Steve asks me.

"No worries."

"And Drongo?"

"A loser or a fool."

"What about flaming galah?"

"Stupid."

He and I use the rest of the break to mingle and drink some water while keeping our fly nets firmly in place. I can feel the heat of the day in the very bones in my body. I gulp more water and have Steve pour a little down my back. It feels so good. A long, cool shower would be wonderful right now. But that's not going to happen.

Steve comments on our parade through town. "That was great. Did you see that big guy punch Brode?"

I smile, "Oh, yes."

"What next?"

"It will depend on what Andre can arrange with Derain. You know your father is going to be livid about all the plane tickets we've had to cancel."

"Wasn't like there was an option."

Andre joins us. "As soon as everyone is back on the camels, we'll separate and head to the cave. Derain will meet us there tomorrow with water bags, supplies, and a map North with the stops marked. He already added sleeping bags and water for us behind our saddles."

"He won't be in any trouble, will he?" I ask.

"If the police ever contact him, he'll say he doesn't know anything. If they press him, he'll say all he knows is that a few camels are missing. My Land Cruiser is already registered in his name. No worries there. His mother is currently wiping our prints off it. I wish we had time for you to meet her. You'd like her. She's a terrific woman."

***

Our luck holds. There's no sign of the police. We turn our camels away from Derain's tourist group and head toward a nearby cave that Andre remembers from his childhood.

I remark how fast the camels are.

Andre says, "Derain's loaned us three from his racing stock. They'll travel faster and further in a day than his normal camels."

I keep scanning the sky for aircraft or drones that might be searching for us. No way we can hide from satellites if Brode manages to get the government involved. We'd be pretty visible if they pass. Hopefully it won't occur to him we chose this way to escape. We've been lucky so far.

I ask Andre "What will you do with the phones?"

"Already done. Remember the abandoned mine shafts we passed coming out of town? I tossed them down one of those."

Good idea, I think. Close to town. If they're found by the police, they'll think we're still near town.

With no cars in sight, we hurry the camels across a road, long past where Ted's mine shaft is caved in, and head to a canyon further into the desert.

***

It's late. The camels sleep, hobbled and blocked inside the cave. Derain said they were fine without water tonight, but they were happy with the grain he packed for them. Steve, exhausted and sore from his first camel ride, has burrowed himself deeply in his sleeping bag. I can hear his slow, deep breaths. Sleep eludes me. My nervous brain won't stop running scenarios for the days ahead.

Andre returns from a check outside. We don't expect any trouble, but better to be safe. He looks from the camels to Steve and back to me.

"You awake? Come," he says. "Bring your sleeping bag. Let's go outside."

CHAPTER THIRTY-FOUR

Andre and I spread our sleeping bags next to the cave entrance which overlooks the canyon entrance and the desert beyond. We snuggle close. Desert nights are cool.

Andre says, "I couldn't take you to my favorite spot, but this is close."

A huge full moon comes up. It climbs into the sky slowly as it has for millennia and will into eternity. The effect is surreal. No wonder Andre loves the desert. I know I'll remember this moment forever.

We sit quietly, letting go of the day's tensions. We could be anywhere in time. There's a primordial feeling here at night. If a tyrannosaurus rex suddenly appeared, I wouldn't be surprised. Freaked out, but not surprised.

Now I understand how people become fascinated with the beauty of the desert. I'm fast becoming one of them.

Andre points out a shooting star. "Make a wish."

Easy. I wish tonight would never end. No more

running, no more death. Just peace.

I've always imagined Andre as an urban bandit, conning his way through European art galleries, gambling in Monaco, and burglarizing mansions in Barcelona. Now I find he's an orphan from Coober Pedy who's at home in the outdoors. What else should I know?

We don't talk much. We need to, but not tonight. I'm terrible at small talk anyway, so we sit in companionable silence.

He leans closer to me and fingers the antique silver cross I always wear. The one he gave to me in Sydney when we were "married."

He slides his arm around my back. His breath tickles my ear as he kisses it. His arms turn me, his lips close over mine, softly at first and then more insistently. I return the kisses with growing ardor. My arms circle his neck. There's no more question. I do love this man. And he must care about me, or he wouldn't offer to go to prison in my place.

***

A noise wakes me during the night. Curious, I listen carefully. Nothing seems out of the ordinary. Not that I would know what is 'ordinary' in the desert. I relax and take in the sky above, marveling again at the brilliant canopy of stars. Andre sleeps peacefully beside me. I snuggle contentedly against his warm body.

***

The early morning light floods the desert landscape as

the sun slowly rises. The air still feels cool on my bare shoulders, but otherwise I'm warm and comfy. I roll over in the sleeping bag to find Andre awake and staring at me from inches away.

"Do you have any idea how beautiful you are?"

I know better, but I'm glad he thinks so.

"Marry me," he says.

"Last time we did that, it didn't work out very well."

"Not because I didn't love you."

"How would it be different this time?"

"What if I went straight?"

"You would do that?"

"If it's the only way I can be with you."

He turns my hands over and kisses my open palms. A flash of heat burns through me.

"Have you ever tried to go straight before?"

"I never knew you before."

My entire being yearns to say yes. I think he means it, but I can guess how it would be. Maybe a year of absolute bliss followed by restlessness, regrets, and unhappiness. And then what? He could be arrested or killed at any moment. I don't think he can exist outside his criminal world any more than I can give up catching crooks. It's our natures. Even if we managed to survive together, we'd come to hate each other. I can't think of anything worse.

I try to explain my reasoning.

Andre brushes it aside. "I could never hate you."

But I know he would eventually. I couldn't live with that. I shake my head sadly. I can't begin to picture him happy working a nine-to-five job.

"Don't say no now," he says quietly. "Think about it." His mouth closes over mine. Rational thoughts disappear as his fingers glide over my body, leaving heat radiating on my skin wherever he touches it.

"Hey, you guys awake yet?" Steve calls from the cave entrance.

Andre and I hastily separate.

"Can you tell me the plan now?" Steve says.

Plan? "Give us a minute," I say. All my doubts and worries about the situation flood back as I hastily re-button my clothes under cover of the sleeping bag.

Once we're presentable, Andre and I join Steve in the cave. We check the camels. They seem content behind the temporary barrier we built of dead branches and bushes we scavenged from the area. Andre gives them each a handful of grain.

Digging through the provisions Derain packed, we find water for us and energy bars. Coffee would be nice, but beggars definitely can't be choosers. Smoke from a fire could easily give away our location.

"Come on," Steve says. "Tell me."

"We're going to camp our way north to Uluru Rock. It's about four hundred and fifty miles plus or minus as a crow flies. Or I could say -- as a fly flies. If all goes well, it will take several weeks. As soon as we get close, Andre will contact Derain. He'll meet us with our real passports and the new set of fake ones. He'll ship his camels home."

"Why don't we just drive to Uluru? It'd be faster."

"Because we'd never get past the police checkpoints. Derain shouldn't have any trouble or raise any interest. There are camel tours in Uluru, too. Crossing the desert at night moves us past the checkpoints. Brode won't know what direction we went in or how."

"But what then? We'll still be stuck in the middle of Australia."

"After that, it's up to Andre."

Andre says, "I ordered tickets for us using fake names to join up with one of the commercial bus tours heading back from Uluru to Darwin. Once in Darwin, we'll meet a friend of mine who owns a fishing boat. He'll take us from Darwin toward Indonesia. If we make it to one of the islands in that area, we can catch a plane home."

Jean steps into the cave carrying a Sig Sauer pistol - aimed at us. Her voice interrupts, "Good plan. It might even have worked."

We're stunned.

Finally, Andre takes a step toward her. "Hi, Jean. Nice -_"

"Stop right there," she says, waving him back toward the camels with her pistol. "Let's not make this tedious."

"You're Riley's partner?" I say. Not for a second had I

231

thought she was involved.

"Only as long as he was useful. Which wasn't going to be much longer anyway. The money was burning a hole in his pocket. He was going to attract attention soon with all his crazy spending."

"I thought Riley and Joan...?" says Steve.

"That was a last resort, in case we couldn't get control of the mine any other way."

"You'd do that to your own sister?" Andre asks.

She shrugs. "I had to plan for my future. Riley? He couldn't even manage to rob a bank."

"So it was you and Riley at the bank? Not Ted?" Andre realizes.

"No, Ted discovered Riley stole his gun and followed Riley to the bank. Ted tried to stop him. It was Riley who shot the guard," she says. "Now, I'd like the box of opals you took from Riley's truck."

"All this is about greed?" Andre asks.

"Why not? I'm owed some of the good things in life."

"And Joan?" I say.

"She wasn't going to miss that mine if she never even knew it existed."

I can see Andre measuring distances with his eyes. Not good. He's too far away from Jean. Unfortunately, Jean notices his intentions, too.

"Don't even think about it, Andre." She increases the distance between them by moving closer to me. I hold my breath she doesn't notice.

"Brode even offered me a nice reward for turning you in." Jean smirks at me. "I am sorry to see your black eye fading. I rather enjoyed seeing it."

"That was you in the closet?" I bristle.

She smiles. "My only regret is I couldn't find the papers. Ted should have given them to me, but he fell and hit his head. Saved me killing him, but it didn't help me any. I couldn't let him come back to Coober Pedy. He would have ruined everything."

"He fell?" I ask.

"I may have given him a shove."

"Too bad you didn't do a better search. Steve found them."

"I wondered how you learned about the mine. Locating the papers would have saved me a lot of time. What I really want to know is how you figured out it was me and followed me to Coober Pedy?"

"We didn't have a clue," Steve says. "Since there were no leads, Lexi decided to follow Ted's casket. If you hadn't tried to kill her with that snake, we would never have known we were in the right place."

"I'll have to remember that," Jean says. "Enough stalling. Where are the opals?"

She notices Andre move closer to her. There's fury in his eyes.

"I always felt there was something wrong with you," he

says. "You have no heart."

She aims her Sig Sauer at him as he steps closer.

Sensing her attention shift, I tackle her - taking both of us down hard.

Bam! Her gun goes off. Andre crumbles.

The gunshot echoes off the walls. Confined in a small space, the noise panics the camels. One hurdles our small containment barrier in fright and then crashes into Jean and I. Jean loses her grip on the gun. Steve leaps for the camel's halter and drags it to a halt.

Jean and I struggle to our feet. She tries to reach her gun on the cave floor. I manage to kick it further away. The camel swings its rear end, shoving me aside, and knocking Jean off her feet. Her head hits the rock wall with a sickening thud. I watch, frozen in horror as her body slides to the ground.

In the sudden silence, the only sound is Steve trying to calm the camel.

I reach Jean and feel for her pulse. Only there isn't any. One minute she was vitally alive and then she's gone. It's still impossible for me to comprehend how fast death can be. And I never believed in poetic justice before -- that she should die the same way as Ted. By a blow to the head? Accident or karma?

I hurry to where Andre lies sprawled. There's blood on his arm. Please don't be dead, please don't be dead. I kneel beside him and search for his pulse. It throbs strongly beneath my fingers. Relief surges through me.

"Is this going to be a thing, Cherie? Why is it, I only get shot when I'm with you?" Andre asks as he sits up. He tries to reassure me. "It's okay. It's only a flesh wound."

In my happiness that he's alive, I kiss him so hard that I almost knock him down again.

"Hey, how about a little help over here?" Steve yells, still trying to hang on to the frightened, bellowing camel. The camel raises its head, dangling Steve in the air.

I jump up to help him. Between the two of us, we manage to guide the fractious animal back behind the barrier with the other jittery camels.

"Good job, Steve," I say. "Without that camel, we'd be up the creek."

"The way that camel's groaning and moaning, you'd think he was the one who got shot," says Andre.

Steve and I give each of the camels a bit of grain to distract them. They stay edgy, but settle a bit.

Relieved, I return to Andre. With Steve's help, I wash and bandage his arm. Luckily the bullet just grazed his upper arm, leaving a bloody, but insignificant wound. While we work, we ignore the 'elephant' in the room. Jean's body.

Finally we're forced to face what happened. Jean's death and her revelations. I take a blanket and cover her body. The three of us move outside and sit near the cave entrance in silence. Words don't come.

I'm emotionally overwhelmed by events. I think Steve

is in shock. Andre's harder to read. Jean was his friend. I can see the anger in his posture at her actions against his other friends. Joan and Emily, who are dear to him. Ted's death, his closest childhood friend. And Riley, used as a pawn, only to be thrown away. It's impossible to comprehend Jean's rationalization.

The thing I'll never understand is Jean's frightening indifference to the lives of her family and friends or her callous motivation.

CHAPTER THIRTY-FIVE

We sit outside the cave entrance for a while before Steve breaks the silence.

"What now?"

"We continue with our plan," Andre says.

"And Jean?" I ask.

"We bury her," he says. "Better for Gale and Joan to wonder what happened to her than for them to ever learn the truth."

Sadly, I can't think of a better solution. The truth would devastate Joan and Gale. I ask, "Is there a shovel in the gear Derain gave us?"

"Yes," answers Steve. "There's a collapsible camping one."

"Wait," I say. "We're missing something. How did Jean find us?"

***

We bury Jean out in the desert away from the cave and

cover her grave with stones to protect it. I wonder about the irony that we're protecting a predator's body from predators. This seems to be my day for weird abstract thinking.

Andre and I take the risk and ride back to the road. We find Jean's car. Inside, I discover a topographical map of caves in the area. Several were crossed out.

"Look at this," I show Andre.

"When we were kids, we used to off-road out here. She must have guessed we put my knowledge of the local caves to use."

After some anxious moments, we decide she wouldn't have told Brode until she found a way to silence us and retrieve the opals.

While I manage the camels, Andre disposes of Jean's car in a deep ravine. When he's finished, we quickly return to the cave.

Once there, we sit down with Steve to wait for Derain's arrival.

CHAPTER THIRTY-SIX

Our trip to Uluru was slow, but my constant anxiety left it blurred in my memory because the days became monotonous.

Derain showed up on schedule with supplies for us packed on an additional camel. He included a map that showed the safest way north and included watering places for the camels. He was wonderful to step up with so much help. To me, it says good things about Andre that his friends are always willing to help him, even when it's a risk to themselves.

This trip has made me question a lot of my beliefs. Like Andre. I don't know a nicer, kinder man. If I didn't know he was a thief, hunted by the law in several countries, I'd agree to marry him in a heartbeat. And Joan. What good would come from telling Joan that Ted embezzled money to pay for her health care. To me, that was a case of morally right versus legally right. I tend to think of things as black or white, but now I'm learning how much of life falls into gray areas.

We left for Uluru as soon as it was dark. We'd sleep during the day, eat, and ride by night -- only to sleep, eat, and ride again. The part I found I didn't mind repeating was spending time with Andre.

Andre continued to call Steve by his actual name instead of kid or boy. They seemed to bury the hatchet. Luckily not in each other's back.

It's also a funny time for Andre and me. Imagine you're in high school and the hot quarterback has asked you out. You're so excited, until your mother insists you take your younger brother with you.

After all that happened in Coober Pedy, it was good to have the time to quietly reflect. It made me come to a decision. I am no longer going to let Morgan hold my job over my head to make me do whatever he wants. He's done it twice now. Next time he tries it, I'm going to walk. Maybe I will have to flip burgers. At least it's an honest, useful living.

Derain met us again near Uluru and took his camels home in a trailer. We made our connections with the tour company and traveled to Darwin by air conditioned bus. The bus was so comfortable, we slept most of the way. Whenever we hit a police road block, the tour bus was waved through. I was surprised the police were still looking for us.

In Darwin, we were met by Andre's friend, who smuggled us onto his boat the night we arrived. We left port the next morning.

I learned professional fishing is hard work and very boring. The three of us ended up with cracked and blistered hands, bad sunburns, and aching backs. Steve spent most of the time leaning over the boat's side being seasick. Andre had a run-in with a tuna that left him with a gash on his leg. The crew had the mistaken idea that because I'm a woman, I could cook. After two nights, I was relieved of that duty.

I hope to never see a yellow fin tuna or a Spanish mackerel again. It was with a sigh of relief, that we stepped off the boat and onto the island country of East Timor, formally known as Timor-Leste. If we could board a plane quickly, we would finally be safe. Detective Inspector Brode wouldn't be able to touch us. I don't think he has any grounds to extradite me or Steve from the U.S. He'll have to locate Andre to extradite him from where ever he ends up.

Since Andre is persona non grata in the U.S., his flight leaves for Greece and unknown points beyond. I hate telling him goodbye. Although our escape from Brode has been a special time, we still haven't found a solution to moving our relationship forward. I'm starting to wonder if that's even possible.

As Steve and I board our plane for home, Andre takes

me in his arms to kiss me passionately. I'm torn. I want so badly to stay with him even knowing it will never work. But finally I force myself to push away.

"Cherie," he says. "This isn't over. I will convince you to marry me."

Hmm, I think. I heard something similar last time we parted, before he disappeared for a year. We'll see.

CHAPTER THIRTY-SEVEN

I yawn. It's early, but when I finally arrived home last night, I found dozens of emails from Jeff. I'm not looking forward to turning him down, but it's unfair to let him wait any longer. We arranged to meet for coffee this morning before I go into the bank.

I take a shower before I leave, but every so often, I catch a whiff of camel or mackerel. Not the most pleasant of smells. Maybe there's an old perfume in my desk at work. I hope so.

Jeff's already waiting when I arrive at the restaurant. He picks up our coffees and bagels at the counter and brings them back to our table.

"Nice to have you back," he says. "How was the trip?"

"Same-old, same-old," I say. "Lots of deceit, murder, and bushwhacking."

He laughs, not taking me seriously. "I told you forensic accounting was going to be boring."

I smile. "You have no idea..."

"Look, I have something important to ask you.

I cringe. I hate that this might be the end of our friendship.

"I've been thinking about this a long time," he says. "I like to plan ahead. I'm going to retire in a few years. What would you think about you and me opening a P.I. firm? Sound interesting? I guarantee it'll be more fun than computers and numbers."

Not a marriage proposal. A business proposal. I'm so relieved, I start to laugh. And I can't stop laughing.

Jeff finally whacks me on the back in concern.

"Yes," I manage to say between bursts of laughter.

***

I'm back in the office less than thirty minutes later when --

"Lexi, get up here. Now!" Morgan yells over my phone.

Sounds like he's feeling like his old self.

I've just stepped into my office and slipped my feet into my crocodile slippers. Is he in that much of a hurry to fire me? I hate to admit it, but I am going to miss working here. I glance around and sigh. It'll be another five to ten years before Jeff actually retires and we can start our own firm.

I touch the beautiful opal ring on my finger. It makes Andre feel close when I do. I miss him already. How long will it be this time before I hear from him again?

I notice several papers in the in-tray of my fax machine.

I wasn't expecting anything. Since I'm not in the mood to rush to Morgan's office, I carry them to my desk to read.

The fax is from Joan. That's a surprise. I know Andre already called her about the mine and Riley. Hmm. I read on.

"Andre told me that Ted borrowed three million from his boss to pay my hospital bills. Please send me details. I want to repay him. I'm fielding astronomical offers for Ted's mine. I'm already in negotiations with a company --"

What exciting news. She and Emily will have financial security. At least Andre used the word borrowed and not stole.

This day is going to be better than I expected. With luck, I won't even get fired if she's going to repay Mac's money.

I head for Steve's cubicle. I can't wait to share the news with him. After that, I'll go tell Morgan.

Steve's phone rings as I reach his door. I pause and hear him say, "Hi Skylar...I apologize, but this just isn't working out...Please stop yelling...That's not going to change my mind..."

I tiptoe away. Probably not a good time. I'll go see Morgan. If all goes well, I'll take the afternoon off to go pick up Frosty. Why I'm taking on a dog, I don't know. I guess I can't bear the idea of him having nowhere to go. If I don't get fired, Frosty and I may even get to enjoy living together. I do love dogs. Somehow I'll make it work.

Olivia, our receptionist, waves me down as I pass her.

"Welcome back, Lexi. Have a good trip?"

"It was definitely an interesting one."

"A special delivery envelope came for you this morning. Do you want it now or shall I send it to your office?"

"I'll take it. Thanks." There's no sender shown. I slit it open. Inside is a plane ticket to Aruba and a brochure for an all inclusive ocean front resort.

Andre, I think. Two weeks of a real vacation with him with no worries. No camels or mackerels either. How wonderful.

The End

If you enjoyed ***Bushwhacked in the Outback***
and would like to leave a review, go to:
http://amazon.com/dp/????

If you missed ***Land Sharks – A Swindle in Sumatra***
(Book 1), go to:
http://amazon.com/dp/B0794M2Q3M/

Lexi, Steve, and Andre will be back soon with a
new adventure. For updates, go to:
http://NancyRavenSmith.com/

ACKNOWLEDGEMENTS

Few authors complete a book alone. Publishing a book takes a "village" that includes beta readers, publishers, editors, agents, cover artists, friends, and family to name a few. Bushwhacked in the Outback is no exception. Here are the wonderful, gifted people who helped, supported. and gave me the space to write.

An enthusiastic thanks to my family, Brad Smith and Lynn Raven for their unfailing love and support of my work. And my extended family, Russ and Opal Raven, and Chloe Hanko for their participation in making this book a reality.

Bushwhacked in the Outback could not have been realized without the critical input from its wonderful Beta Readers -- Nancy Stehman, Janice Metz, and Judy Metz.

I'd also like to thank the Best Page Forward Team for their special help.

My heartfelt thanks to you all for your continued support.

BOOKS BY NANCY RAVEN SMITH

Land Sharks - A Swindle in Sumatra

A Cozy Mystery Adventure
(Book 1)

by Nancy Raven Smith
https://www.amazon.com/dp/B0794M2Q3M/

"Land Sharks is one of the best mysteries I have read in a long time...A great mystery woven into an area which I have traveled...Strongly recommend this read!"
- An Amazon Reader

"I loved this book! I hated to put this book down. The touch of romance added to the mystery. The descriptions of the jungle were so vivid it was easy to feel as if you were there with Lexi! An interesting character and can't wait for the next book. Now that she has Steve as a partner I wonder how things work on their next investigation!"
- An Amazon Reader

The Reluctant Farmer of Whimsey Hill
by
Bradford Smith with Lynn Raven and Nancy Raven Smith

https://www.amazon.com/dp/B01H0MCVIE/

"Animals can and do make our lives better. This is my kind of book."
- Bret Witter, #1 New York Times best selling co-author of *Dewey* [the Library Cat]"

"A witty memoir reminding us that the best lessons in life are beyond the edge of one's comfort zone, and one can only be towed there by the heart strings."
- Jean Abernethy, creator of Fergus the Horse
The Reluctant Farmer of Whimsey Hill is an animal lover's delight, but there is so much more; love, family, friendship, humor, sadness and just good reading. [The authors] have joined forces and written a perfectly delightful book that was impossible to put down. I cannot say enough good things about *The Reluctant Farmer of Whimsey Hill.* I highly recommend it to everyone young and old; male and female; you will not be disappointed.
- Reviewed By Trudi LoPreto for *Readers' Favorite - 5 Stars*

INTERESTING FACTS ABOUT COOBER PEDY

Coober Pedy (Kupa Piti) - The name is translated from the Aboriginal phrase as "white man in a hole."

Olympic Australis - The largest and most valuable opal was found in Coober Pedy's Eight Mile opal fields in 1956 at the time the Australian Olympic Games. It was named Olympic Australis in honor of the games. The stone weighs 17,000 carats and has been valued at $2,5000,000 AU dollars ($1,900,000 USD).

Golf Course - The Coober Pedy Opal Fields Golf Club does have a real, physical golf course. Members mostly play at night to escape the heat and use neon balls. There is no grass on the course. Golfers are given a square of turf to carry with them and use for teeing off. Members also have reciprocal playing rights with St. Andrews in Scotland. A bonus of being a member of the Coober Pedy Club is that you get to keep any opals you find while playing. One golfer found an opal worth $3,500 on the course.

Weather in Coober Pedy, Central AU - The weather ranges from 122 degrees Fahrenheit to sub zero. The interiors of dugouts stay at a steady 73.4 degrees Fahrenheit.

Movies - The Coober Pedy area is popular for shooting

movies, especially for representing Mars and dystopian areas. Here's a partial list of titles: Mad Max III, Pitch Black, Priscilla, Queen of the Desert, Red Planet, Fire In The Stone, Where The Green Ants Dream, Until the End Of the World, Kangaroo Jack, The Drover's Boy, Siam Sunset, Ground Zero.

Opals - Opals can be worth more per carat than diamonds.

The Stuart Highway - It divides Central Australia from Adelaide (Port Augusta) in the South to Darwin in the North. The highway is 2700 kilometers (1677.02 miles) long. There is little to no police supervision. Tractor trailers pulling 3-4 extra trailers form "truck trains" and frequent the highway. Amenities are few.

People - people from more than 44 nationalities live in Coober Pedy. The population is 1,762

Camels - Camels were introduced to Australia in 1840. They were used first by explorers and then by the Australian Military.

ABOUT THE AUTHOR

NANCY RAVEN SMITH is a multi-award winning screenwriter and author. Her first mystery, Land Sharks - A Swindle in Sumatra, was chosen as an Amazon/Kindle Scout Program Selection. Born under the zodiac water sign Cancer, she loves super-soaker fights, warm beaches, hot bubble baths, and white water rafting.

Her mysteries are filled with humor, adventure, and romance set in exotic locations. Originally from Virginia, she and her husband now reside in Southern California - and yes, they live near the water.

Raven Smith's memberships include Sisters in Crime, Mystery Writers of America, and Women in Film. She advocates for animal rescue.